^{THE} Afterlife

Also by Gary Soto

THE Afterlife

GARY SOTO

HARCOURT, INC.

Orlando   Austin   New York   San Diego   Toronto   London

Requests for permission to make copies of any part of the work should be
mailed to the following address: Permissions Department, Harcourt, Inc.,
6277 Sea Harbor Drive, Orlando, Florida 32887-6777.

www.HarcourtBooks.com

Library of Congress Cataloging-in-Publication Data
Soto, Gary.
The afterlife / Gary Soto.
p.   cm.
Summary: A senior at East Fresno High School lives on as a ghost after
his brutal murder in the restroom of a club where he has gone to dance.
1. Mexican Americans—Juvenile fiction.   [1. Mexican Americans—Fiction.
2. Ghosts—Fiction.   3. Murder—Fiction.   4. California—Fiction.]   I. Title.
PZ7.S7242Af   2003
[Fic]—dc21   2003044995
ISBN 0-15-204774-3

Text set in Dante
Designed by Linda Lockowitz

First edition
H   G   F   E   D   C   B   A

Printed in the United States of America

APR 1 3 2004

For Chanah Cossman and Mark Lasher,
Health Providers of West Fresno

^{THE} Afterlife

CHAPTER
One

WHEN YOU'RE an ordinary-looking guy, even *feo,* you got to suck it up and do your best. You got to shower, smell clean, and brush your teeth until the gums hurt. You got to dress nice and be Señor GQ. You got to have a little something in your wallet. You got to think, *I'll wow the chicas with talk so funny that they'll remember me.* This was my lover-boy strategy as I stood in the restroom of Club Estrella combing my hair in the mirror over the sink. I was going to meet Rachel at the dance—Rachel, the girl in the back row in English, the one whose gum-snapping chatter made Mrs. Mitchell's brow furrow. I shook water from my comb and plucked the teeth like a harp. I brought the comb back into my hair again. I had to get it right.

It was from happiness, I guess, that I turned to the guy next to me. I said I liked his shoes. They were yellow and really strange to a dude like me who clopped about in imitation Nikes but on that night was wearing a pair of black shoes from Payless. I looked back at the mirror and noticed a telephone number carved with a key in the corner—265-3519. I let my mind play: I could call that number. I could say, "Your number's on the mirror, girlie." I pictured someone like Rachel answering and roaring a frosty, "So!" Then she would be cool, come on strong, and ask, "What's your name, tiger? What's your school? What kind of ride you got?"

Ride? I had a bicycle with a bent rim and a skateboard from junior high somewhere in the garage. But a ride? It was Payless shoes made of plastic. Shoes I was going to toss in the closet once the night was over.

But the private world inside my head disappeared quickly. The guy next to me, the one with the yellow shoes, worked an arm around my throat, snakelike, and with his free hand plunged a knife into my chest. He stuck me just left of my heart, right where I kept an unopened pack of Juicy Fruit gum—I had intended to sweeten my breath later when I got Rachel alone. I groaned, "No way," and touched that package of gum as I turned and staggered. He lunged and stuck me a second time, just above my belly button—blood the color of pomegranate juice spread across my shirt. I thought, *This is not me,* and leaned against a sink, grimacing because that one hurt. My legs buckled as I turned and straightened when he stuck me in my lower back. I cried, "How come?" I saw myself in the mirror, my breath on the glass, a vapor that would disappear. I breathed on the surface and saw, in the reflection, the guy stepping away and looking at the ground as if he had dropped a quarter. Then, chin out, he stepped toward me, pulled out the shirttail from the back of my pants, and wiped his blade.

"What did you say to me, *cabrón?*" he breathed in my ear. He smelled of a hamburger layered with onions.

My answer was on the glass. It was a blot of my breath, a blot of nothing. I couldn't form a word because of how much I hurt.

The guy in yellow shoes pushed me away. He put his penknife into his shirt pocket like it was a pen or pencil. He pulled a paper towel from the dispenser, and wiped his face as if his meanness could be stripped away. He coughed once. I could have used some of that air he was exhaling—I was starting to pant, worried because my lungs couldn't fill.

He inspected his hands and discovered freckles

of blood on his knuckles. His thumb erased some of the freckles. He washed his hands in the basin and left the water running.

"You hurt me," I groaned, then collapsed to the floor, where I lay curled up, blood pouring evenly from three holes. When I swallowed, I tasted blood. Blood rolled over the lenses of my eyes. My body began to shudder, and I wanted to stop it, but how?

"So?" he hissed, and flicked the wadded-up paper towel at me. He pulled open the door, and the last I saw of him were his yellow shoes. I pillowed my head on my arm, moaned. The floor was cold and dirty, with tracks of shoe prints. It was the territory of mice and cockroaches, but I was neither. I closed my eyes. When I opened them a minute later, I was dead.

MY NAME IS Jesús, named after my father, whose own father was Maria Jesús, born in the 1940s in Jalisco, Mexico. But I was known as Chuy at East Fresno High. There was nothing really special about me—I ran cross-country, ate my lunch with friends, and with those same friends, all average looking like me, crowded around the fountain eyeing girls. It had been a good life until now.

As I rose out of my body, I realized that the pain was gone. But so was my last year in high school. So was the fall dance, my time with Rachel, who was not yet *mi novia*—my girl—but might have been if I could have brought her into my arms and convinced her that I was one marvelous thing. That evening I would have had every chance. After all, I had borrowed my uncle Richard's Honda, which was tricked-out and lowered like a cat, with ten-inch speakers in the panels and clear lights that cut a path on dark streets. My uncle, only seven years older than me, was a true guy—he had filled up the gas tank for me, vacuumed the floor mats, and run a rag over the dash. He had even replaced the air freshener, a tiny cardboard tree that swayed under the dash when later I took a sharp corner, tires chirping. The wind of those turns helped scent the air with pine.

When my friend Angel and I came to pick up his car, Uncle Richard tossed the keys at me and then put me in a headlock. "You dent my ride, and I'll kill you!" he threatened with a mean smile, and maybe meant it. But someone else had killed me first, the guy in yellow shoes, and I hadn't even driven more than ten miles in Uncle Richard's ride—the gas tank was still full.

This was a Friday night on what had been an ordinary October, and the first pumpkins were being set out on porches. Families, I suspected, were already buying five-pound bags of candies for the troops that would show up in a week. Leaves were falling, and the lawns were growing more damp every night. The chilly mornings put people in sweaters and coats.

But I was not going to be around for Halloween, the last year, I had vowed, that I would go trick-or-treating. Me and some friends had intended to put on masks and go door-to-door, croaking in our teenage voices, "Trick or treat." If the homeowners had ripped off our masks, they would have discovered boys that were really men. My good friend Jason, in fact, already had a beard.

But I wasn't going to be around. On that Friday night, I rose from my body and wavered like smoke and stared at *myself* crumpled on the floor. My wounds were gashes that resembled the gills of fish searching for air. They were still pulsating as blood seeped and flowed to the right corner of the restroom. The floor was red, sticky. I remembered a time I spilled strawberry Kool-Aid when I was little, maybe six, and trying to show *mi papi* that I was a big man—big enough to carry the pitcher to the kitchen table. But I spilled the Kool-Aid, and he spanked me because I did bad.

But what bad had I done now? I rose like a ghost. I gazed at my body, the pile that was my young skin and hard bones. My eyes were open, but they couldn't see me, for the light behind them was gone. My fingers were curled, as if I was ready for a fight. But there was no fight in me. I felt shame because I noticed the crotch of my pants was wet. Did that happen during the stabbing, or in death? It must have been after I died that my bladder released its water. I prayed that was how the body worked when you're brought down with a blade. I hated the thought that my father would pull back the sheet and look at me, his son with legs splayed and presenting a wet crotch for all to see. The shame of dying during one last piss.

A ghost with the weight of a zero, I rose still higher. My body was lean because I was seventeen, a long-distance runner for the school, and a Saturday weight lifter in my garage. I was also an occasional brick hauler for my dad, a mason for the city who sometimes got jobs on the side. I worked side by side with my dad, his only child, shouldering bags of cement from the pickup truck to backyards.

The ghost that was me hovered over my body and watched a guy come into the restroom rapping words to a song about a street killer. I'm sure he thought he was sweet, all *suave,* as he spun his own made-up rap song about death and drive-bys. But his off-key singing stopped. His mouth became an open sack when he saw me—my body, I mean—and saw that he had accidentally stepped in a puddle of my blood. He made a face at his shoes, black ones just like mine, and scraped them against the floor to rid them of bloody tracks that would follow him out of the restroom, tracks that would quickly grow faint with each step. He left the restroom in a hurry. He called the name Julio three times, each time a little louder, with greater urgency, as if he were the one stuck, not me. Who was Julio but a friend, a *carnal*, who tagged along with him that evening. Dudes, like *chicas*, never show up at dances alone; they go in pairs and return home in pairs unless one of them gets lucky. Like Angel and me. Angel was my friend on the dance floor, circling like a shark and resembling a shark—he had pointed teeth and hair that stood up like a fin. But he was a good dude, really, though more desperate than me to swing into the arms of a girl. And he was uglier than me, plus a little bit chubby around the middle.

I was waiting for Julio and the guy with my blood on the soles of his shoes to return. *They'll come in*, I thought, *and help me to my feet*, even if it meant getting blood on their shirts and ruining the evening for them. They'll call an ambulance—one of them had to have a cell phone. But before people rushed in to see about the noise, I saw my body quiver one more time. *Dang*, I thought. *I'm going. I'm growing cold.* I imagined the cold traveling up my throat to my face and pressing against my eyes. They would close, and I would really be dead.

Suddenly my ghost settled back in my body, and for a moment I felt myself breathe—my legs shuddered, then stilled, and I let out a hiss like the sound of a tire going flat. I had returned to life, and then died a second time.

I felt myself—the ghost, I mean—again slip from my bones and drift toward the ceiling. I thought: *What's happening?* I wanted to hang on to the sink or grip something to keep me at ground level. I wanted to remain next to my body, but I was light now that I had no body for an anchor. I floated toward the rack of fluorescent lights. I drifted through the ceiling, the pink of insulation, and the tarred shingles. I found myself on the roof, the air-conditioning unit of the nightclub roaring. I rose higher, and thought I was going to pee again when I drifted off the roof and hung in the air. I looked down and spied two dudes sparking up in the parking lot. They were leaning on Uncle Richard's Honda. I wanted to holler, "Get your dirty *nalgas* off the car!"

But I whispered to myself, "Man, I'm flying." I felt any second that I was going to drop like a sack of cement and burst open. But I flew and fought my instinct to flap my ghostly arms; after all, isn't that how birds stay in the air? I floated between the nightclub and a boarded-up insurance company, floated above the parked cars, and the dudes and *chicas* at the entrance, all of them trying to get in through double doors smeared with the fingerprints of hairspray, cologne, and adolescent sweat. I recognized my *primo* Eddie, a year older than me at eighteen, a high school dropout studying air-conditioning at City College. *"Primo,"* I called, but he couldn't hear me. I looked up at the sky. The moon was nearly full and dented as a hubcap.

In the distance, the sirens of an ambulance and fire truck were wailing for me. Or, at least, for that body on the bloody floor of a dirty restroom.

THE GRAVITY OF my new status as a ghost began to sink in as I hovered above the roof. I was amazed by this transformation, and by how in my heart I didn't harbor hate for the dude who stuck me. It was weird. He had just taken my life, but I wasn't angry with him. In real life, people would just look at me and I would get mad. But where was my anger now? Maybe in death all that goes. And fear, too. I wasn't scared at all.

I watched the sky until the dark paled and the sun rose pink as a scar. By then the night wind that flaps laundry and trees had vanished. *La chota*—the police—had come and gone, along with the ambulance that carried my body to wherever the dead are bathed and tidied up before they are lowered into the ground. My uncle came and picked up his Honda, and I saw him hammer the steering wheel with his palm. He buried his face into the steering wheel, sobbing. He drove away, scattering the leaves that had gathered around his tires.

The cops returned, too. They went inside the club and half an hour later came out with the owner, an older man with watery eyes named Manuel Something-or-other. He appeared sad, and even sadder when he shook a cop's hand.

"I'm sorry," I heard the owner mumble.

The cops left, taking with them some testimony. But the testimony was with me, not the owner. I was the one killed. And I didn't feel even as bitter as aspirin. It was all weird.

My father and mother didn't show up, though I knew they were probably crying in the shadows of our house in southeast Fresno, homeland for Mexicans and Hmongs mostly. I pictured my parents. They were in the living room, the light of the television sparkling off their eyeglasses. I pictured my mother turning her head when the telephone rang and rising slowly from the couch with a groan, the crocheted afghan on her lap falling to the floor. She would mutter something about the stupid telephone ringing just as the program was getting good, and scold her *viejo*—her old man, my father— for not answering it. Her face would become a mess of lines, and her mouth would tighten into a bud, then loosen as the voice on the other end told her that I had been killed. I pictured her dropping the phone and bringing a knuckle to her mouth. Then my father, heavy as cement, having inhaled so much of it, would turn his camel-large head. He would rise from his recliner to pick up the telephone and scream over the noise of the television, *"Cómo?"*

Still, I was surprised they didn't come to at least circle the place where I had died. Everybody panicked when the cops first came. They had their nightsticks drawn and bullied their way into the dance hall. The police had shoved a couple of dudes against the wall, and arrested one wobbly-legged scarecrow when he couldn't manage to swallow a storm cloud of marijuana. The cloud floated from his mouth, and, high on *mota,* he had been pushed into a cruiser in the parking lot.

"This is a trip," I said to myself, and screamed it from the roof. People were passing below but they couldn't hear me. I screamed my name, and no one—not even a stray dog that was kicking down the street—could hear me. I was learning about my new self.

I could see the outline of myself, which was sort of like a figure penciled in and then erased on paper. I was vaguely visible to myself, but invisible to others—two workers on the roof on the next building were doing something to the gutters. I waved my arms, but they couldn't see me. They kept jamming a garden hose down one of the gutters as they started to blast away leaves and crap.

"It's a trip." I formed the words on my lips. "I'm a ghost."

My wounds were closed, my Juicy Fruit gum still in my shirt pocket. Then a horn blasted, and I jumped, scared, and drifted off the roof like a balloon, slowly descending to the street. I touched down on the sidewalk, amazed that there was nothing to it—just float off a building and land softly. Ever since I was a little dude out of my diapers, I had dreamed of flying, and I guess now that dream was coming true.

Plus, I was invisible. A man tripping down the street couldn't see me—he was shoving a twenty-dollar bill into his wallet. He walked past me and hissed playfully at a stray cat hugging the dried bushes of that closed-down insurance company. The cat was carrying something gray in its mouth. A mouse? A pigeon that wasn't quick enough?

Dead, with my eyes wide open, I began a new life without a body. I had nothing to fear.

DOWNTOWN FRESNO. I floated into Longs Drugs right through the plate glass and positioned myself over the head of a cashier, her eyes narrow as hatchets as she announced over the intercom, "Rafael, code fourteen, aisle six." I knew the meaning of the code—a shoplifter was sliding something under his jacket. I glanced up at the sign posted above aisle six: shampoo and hair care products. My bad. A teenage girl out to improve her looks was snagging one thing or another, and I would have kicked down that aisle except I confronted my uncle Richard and my cousin Eddie—Richard was cradling flowers in his arms and Eddie had large bags of barbecue potato chips under his arms as if they were pillows. Their steps were slow, as if they were wading in water. Their eyes were puffy, their faces dark from not shaving.

"*Tío*," I called. I pointed a finger at my chest. "*Primo*, it's me."

They couldn't hear me. They passed through my outstretched arms and headed to the cashier, whose hatchet eyes had become sharper.

I had never seen Uncle Richard with flowers before, but then again I had never seen him cry before, like he did early this morning in his Honda. They were going to visit my parents, I realized, and they believed it was smart of them to bring something sweet-smelling to my mom. And the potato chips? Snacks for the ride over.

At my parents' house, there would be others to lament my death at such a young age. Angel, *mi carnal*, would be there, with the cement bags of guilt on his shoulders. *I should have been with him*, he would argue with himself. *We could have took the dude!* "He

14

would be alive," he would cry, and I would cry in return, "*Chale,* we would both be dead!" In the three fights that I seen Angel in, he had lost them all. The guy was just a chubby, peace-loving dude.

I stood between Richard and Eddie. Richard said, "I feel weird." He rubbed his arm with his free hand.

Right then, I understood my power. I was dead, but I could offer a chill as cold as ice.

Eddie looked toward the ceiling. "It's the air-conditioning. It's set too cold."

They bought their goodies and were out the door just as the cashier cried into the intercom, "Rafael, code fourteen, aisles seven, nine, and fourteen."

Incredible, I thought. *People lifting the whole store.*

CHAPTER
Two

I PICKED UP right away that the dead can move with speed. For me, each step was nearly twice as long as my usual stride. However, if you're in the air flying, you hardly moved at all. You sort of strolled with your legs churning like you were on a bicycle. I giggled because it was a trip, me striding down the street and away from Longs Drugs, where I imagined the shoplifters scattering like chickens, stolen goods falling from their jackets and blouses— hair dye, lipstick, and bags of candies for those who couldn't wait for trick or treat! I was going somewhere on my own sweet time, and I was bouncing, almost leaping. I thought: *Man, I could have used this on the basketball court.* Me slamming the rock into a bent hoop with a ragged net. Then I would have made the team!

I learned immediately that I couldn't pick things up. When I saw a quarter winking at me in the morning sunlight, I bent down to pocket that little piece of change. But my hand shoved right into the sidewalk.

"Damn," I crowed as I stood up with a jerk. I studied my hand and wiggled my fat thumb that was bishop to all the rest of my fingers. I laughed at myself because what was I going to do with a quarter anyway? Help some poor soul whose parking meter had expired?

I next put my hand right through a tree trunk and a car window. I used a karate chop on a bus bench and shoved a hand through a newspaper rack. For fun, I socked the stucco wall of a church on Mariposa Street. The church was for sale—Jesus, I suppose, had moved from that part of downtown Fresno, having had his fill of the poor, who were only half listening on how to get out of the gutter and get on with life.

This much I grasped: I could slip through walls or doors, but none of what I found on the other side could be mine. Figure this: I could step right through a steel-reinforced vault and sniff all the hundred-dollar bills I wanted, but I couldn't walk away with any of that *feria*.

The second thing I learned was that it was hard to control where I was going. Wind could boss me around, or the breeze of a car or truck could slap me down. I was like a balloon. Sure, I could command myself, "Go there," and I would move in that direction. But I traveled where the slightest wind blew, kicking along with little control. I got pushed to Van Ness Avenue toward the west side—Chinatown, as we call it. But the Chinese had moved out, the Japanese, too, and the blacks with ambition. Now there were only boarded-up stores. Winos, crazies, and the truly poor lingered, their eyes bloodshot from drink and illness. Stray cats lived on Dumpster meals. Pigeons feasted on what people tossed from cars, and they must have tossed a lot, because litter scuttled in the wind. Now and then a family of mice would scale up drainpipes and tumble down with their bellies full from drinking rainwater that gathered on roofs.

Mi familia, I thought. I should kick over to my house and kneel in front of my mother and father. I would tell them, "Mom, it's okay to cry, but it don't hurt no more. And, Mom, I'm sorry for sometimes being stupid and not listening to you about good grades." I would tell my dad, "I'm sorry about the fender on the car—yeah, it was my fault and not the other dude's. I shouldn't have messed up so much."

I loved my parents and wanted to see them. But the wind blew in the direction of the west side! I didn't want to go there!

The morning wind nudged me westward three blocks from Longs Drugs, five from where I was stabbed, and six from the abandoned church on Mariposa Street. Then the wind stopped. I anchored myself in front of Cuca's Restaurant, closed up with a sign that read ON VACATION. I peered in. The kitchen was all shadows, and the booths where *Mexicanos* usually hunkered were empty. A single light in a hallway was on, casting a yellowish glare. The clock on the wall read 9:17. Time was still speeding along in that restaurant, but no one was there to care.

I turned from the window and spied a husky cop across the street frisking a *cholo,* who had his arms raised as if he were praising the pagan god of Don't Move Or Else. I walked over in four long strides, looking neither left nor right for there was no traffic to speak of, except for a dog who was in the middle of the street sniffing a flattened milk carton. I approached the cop and stood so close to him that I could smell the breakfast burrito on his breath. And was that Old Spice cologne, the kind my dad uses? The cop wheeled around and looked directly at me. This spooked me a little, a guy so close I was seeing cross-eyed. He felt something; his sixth sense was in working order. Of course, he couldn't see me. If he whacked me with his nightstick, what harm would result? I had already seen worse.

"Hey," I mouthed.

The cop wrinkled his brow. He could feel my presence.

"Leave the *carnal* alone," I scolded. "Go jump on someone else. Begin with the mayor and work your way down!"

Although I could talk, I couldn't be heard.

The cop licked his lips for moisture. He looked at me, and, like a spear, I plunged a hand right into his chest and felt his heart. It was flabby and clotted with cholesterol. The cop was out of shape. His gut hung over his belt and his muscles were soft as water balloons. The guy must have liked his bacon and his ham thick as shoe leather.

"Ahh," the cop cried, stepping back, his hand over his heart. The badge on his chest sparkled from that electrical charge of my hand coming out, bloodless.

The wiry *cholo* staggered backward, nervous. "I didn't do anything."

He hadn't. He was a little gangster, but that morning, sporting a black hat, he had just been walking across Chinatown to god knows where, his death for all anyone knew. Maybe his luck, like mine, would run out later that day. *Quien sabe?*

The cop examined the front of his shirt, surprised perhaps that his ticker was still thumping. He then winced at the *cholo*.

"Something wrong?" the *cholo* asked meekly, his arms still in the air. His tiny rat eyes were getting smaller. His goatee was twitching, and the tattoo of a snake on his arm was throbbing. The guy was terrified.

"Get out of here!" the cop snarled.

The *cholo*, hand on his hat, hurried away, scaring the dog that was now gripping in his chops the flattened milk carton.

The cop rubbed his chest and got into his cruiser. I followed by the force of my spirit. This was also what I was learning, that to penetrate something solid you had to issue up a little grunt, like opening a heavy door or lifting a sack of my dad's cement. I grunted as my ghostly body lowered itself into the backseat. I smiled. *I'm going somewhere in a police cruiser,* I thought, *and I ain't even in trouble!*

The cruiser pulled away from the curb and the cop raised his attention to the rearview mirror. He was looking at me, but he couldn't see me. It was a trip, me in the backseat and laughing to myself. I have to admit that I had never been in the back of a cruiser before, and assessed the quality of the ride. Kind of nice, I judged. Then we hit a pothole and I sank into the seat and rose violently, my head for a moment jammed through the roof. It was like I was in a tank, my head out and searching the grubby west side passing before my eyes.

The radio squawked and the cop picked up.

"Car twelve," the cop mumbled, his trigger finger on the button.

"Domestic on Yosemite," the dispatcher cracked. "Backup in five."

The cruiser sped up but not by much. And by his groan, I was sure that he was thinking, *Yosemite, crackheads sitting on car fenders. Lazy-ass fathers already popping open their first beers of the day. Why hurry?*

The street was mostly Section Eight apartments with radios and televisions blaring in English and Spanish. Babies in strollers rocked back and forth by slightly older babies. Laundry hanging like the faded flags of defeated nations. The yards were cropped to dirt from bored dogs wagging their sorry tails back and forth. *Why hurry,* the cop probably thought. Maybe he was right. Unless someone got killed. Then he would be wrong.

I hunkered in the back of the cruiser, hands on my lap, as I pretended that I was in a limo. The luxury of a free ride! If only my friends were with me, alive of course. I closed my eyes, then opened them quick, scared awake by the vision of the knife plunging just above my navel. . . .

THE COP WAS backed up by another cop, a Chicano, who was trim in his waist and all rocks in his shoulders. The guy was huge, nothing to play with, a guy

22

so strong he could lift up a car if it, by chance, had rolled onto your foot. I followed the cops into the apartment where, we learned, the previous night a husband had slapped his wife once and not very hard. His wife then crashed a ceramic planter over his head as he slept off his *cruda,* his hangover. And that was the argument. Who was going to clean up the broken pot that lay on the carpeted floor? The plant in it was wilted, the dirt scattered like ashes.

Dawg, I thought. A couple arguing over who's going to pick up the pieces of a broken pot? What about their broken marriage? What about the two babies on the couch, neither of them moving? Were they broken, too?

The cops, invited inside the apartment by the wife, strode across the living room. The fat one snapped off the radio and the muscled one turned down the television, though his eyes sized up a basketball layup—it was Saturday morning and the second week of college hoops. Cal Berkeley was getting a big-time whipping from Arizona.

The two cops gave the husband and wife the once-over, then the babies who were sharing a single bottle. A Chihuahua was shivering under the dining table.

"We have a problem, don't we?" the fat cop asked. There wasn't much confidence in his voice. Perhaps he was still concerned about his heart.

The husband shrugged his shoulders. He munched his lower lip.

"He's messing with that *puta*," the wife scolded. She pointed a hand shaped into a gun. If it had been a gun, her husband would be flying across the living room, in midair and already dead.

"Don't call her that," the husband returned. "Her name is Pumpkin."

The wife's eyes got bigger. Her hand was still shaped like a gun. "I see you with her and I hurt you both!"

The two cops let them have their say for ten long minutes. Then the muscular cop instructed his partner to take the wife and babies outside. The Chihuahua followed, its tin bell tinkling on its collar.

The muscled cop quietly closed the door and, turning, hissed, "Pick up the vase." His chest rose, his jaw hardened.

The husband stubbornly sat in his recliner, an obvious mistake. The cop pulled him up by his wrists and squeezed.

"*Ay, dios,*" the husband cried. His mouth made the sorrowful pout of a fish freed from a hook. He did a little dance when the cop squeezed even harder.

"Pick it up—now!" The cop's eyes were wired with an electrical charge called anger. I figured bolts of lightning would soon be zapping out of his eyes.

He released the husband and threatened, "I should break your ugly *cara!*"

The husband was quickly on the floor scooping up the pieces as if they were gold nuggets. He let the debris rain onto the open face of a newspaper.

"I don't want to come back—*entiendes?*" the cop warned. He glanced around the apartment and his attention was drawn to the water dripping in the kitchen sink. "And I want you to do the dishes after I leave."

When the husband only sobbed, the cop booted him lightly. "The dishes! You understand, *cabrón?*"

This was better than a *telenovela*. I watched the scene while kicking back in the recliner, feet up. I had to agree he was a *cabrón*, a weak-brained guy making a scene in front of his children. And in the apartment complex, the neighbors were probably dunking *pan dulce* into their coffee and gossiping. Such was the pastime of neighbors—all *chismosos* and *chismosas*—with time on their hands.

The husband set another newspaper on the floor. My attention locked onto the news of my death shown there—a photo of me taken in my freshman year. My ears stuck out, almost stupidly, because my head had been shaved at the time. I had always wanted to be mentioned in the newspaper, and finally I was: a three-inch column. I got out of the recliner and was on all fours reading this tidy news of my passing. Three inches was all I got: The story said I was killed at Club Estrella and mentioned that I was a high school long-distance runner. *No más.* Then a single quote from Angel, who lamented, "He just went into the restroom. I'm so angry." Behind that simple pronouncement I could read: He was going to find the guy who did me. Revenge was the flip side of a dirty coin.

Ghosts can't cry. But I learned they can send a chill, and that's what the husband first felt—chills riding down the back of his neck as he stood up, scattering the pieces of the planter funneled in the newspaper. He sensed me. The cop sensed me.

Both took steps away from my cold breath blowing the newspaper. It was fluttering at its edges, actually rising from the floor and scattering the debris.

"Jesus," the cop shouted, his hand reaching for his holster. He unbuckled the leather strap and undid the safety of his gun. The husband backed into the kitchen, scared.

Angel, I thought. *I've got to see my homie!* I pictured him in his cluttered bedroom studying the dry rivers of his palms. I pictured those rivers filling with tears and his hands closing into fists of anger. I could never use a word like *love* for a homie, but that's the kind of language I had in my heart.

I howled my ghostly breath on the newspaper, and the bits of dirt arranged themselves like a beard on my photo. I was dead, I realized, but I could still have my say. I had influence. For all I cared, the no-good husband was going to get religion. Or at least the dishes were going to get done without his old lady getting on his case.

I cruised through the wall, fists first, and down the balcony littered with toys—one was a rubber knife that could bring down a child in a pretend death. Kids practicing for the future.

FROM THE Section Eight apartment, I drifted toward Angel's house, or *tried* to drift, because the October wind blew me westward to Chinatown, where the bars were now open—Mexican *rancheras* were hollering for attention from jukeboxes. A couple of gold-toothed *borrachos* staggered down the street, slurring in Spanish. The dog I had seen earlier was still in the street, this time sniffing a crushed carton of Chinese food. Times were hard, and going to get harder. Three stray cats were having a powwow on the hood of an abandoned car. They were sharing a meal of a pigeon that was now mostly feathers.

Luckily, the wind shifted and sent me eastward, toward Angel's house, off of Tulare Street. I learned that if I tightened my belly, like I was doing a sit-up, I could ground myself. But even then a wind could come up and direct me where I had no interest in going.

I kicked toward Angel's house and found him in the front yard raking leaves. It was Saturday, and death or no death, his *papi,* an ex-Marine who had trooped through the brief Persian Gulf War, expected a clean yard. He expected the car washed, and all the weeds to be yanked from the cracks in the driveway and sidewalk. His family had to set an example for others on the block.

By the movement of the rake, I could tell that Angel's own spirit was sadly deflated. I wanted to stop his sadness, to tell him that it wasn't too bad, to tell him not to be stupid and not to go hunting for the guy who killed me.

"Angel," I called.

Angel poked at the leaves gathered under a bush.

"Angel," I called again. "It ain't all that bad."

His dad appeared on the porch. His eyes were wet, and I realized for the first time that his *papi* was tender underneath his muscular arms and chest. He had been crying over me, his son's best friend. He was crying for every young man who goes down by a violent crime.

"Come in, *mi'jo,*" his father cooed softly.

"In a second," Angel answered, not looking up. If he had, he might have seen a v-shaped formation of geese, something I myself hadn't seen in years. I watched the geese and then turned my attention to Angel's dad. He was staring at his son, and I know that he longed to hug him, to bring him into his body and say, "I'm sorry for Chuy." He pulled at a tear in the corner of his eye, and plucked off the dead head of a rose that had climbed onto their porch. He crumbled the petals, and scattered them in the flower bed. He went back inside, an ex-Marine who was still all rock.

I blew my ghostly breath on the leaves, and the leaves danced a polka, rising ankle high. Angel, somewhat confused, raked them up again. I blew once more, this time sending the leaves fluttering shoulder high, like playing cards tossed in the air.

"What the hell?" Angel muttered. He watched a leaf rock in the air, caught it, and examined it. He looked directly at me, and when I squeezed his shoulder, the pressure of my hand entered his flesh. I touched something at the core of his soul.

"Chuy?" he asked the air.

"Angel," I mouthed. I squeezed and let go.

The rake fell from his hand.

I stepped back. I had so much to tell him, my bro since first grade. But I had no voice other than the icy chill of my breath. I had no other way to reach him than the vague feeling of touch. But he was aware that I stood in front of him.

"Chuy," he said. His eyes filled with the gray waters of sadness.

I laughed to myself. I recalled how he and I had

liked the same girl in fifth grade. We were desperate for love even then because we understood we were not good-looking. Behind Room 34, he and I threw punches at each other, our noses immediately bloody. We were fighting royally over Maya Ramirez all because that afternoon she had glanced our way as we were eating slices of watermelon over a dented trash can. Flies were coming out of the trash can, plus the sour smells of an old hot dog or something. But we were eating our watermelon down to the rind when she smiled flirtatiously. *"Hijole!"* we yelled, juice running from the corners of our mouths. Later that week, we had a pushing match on the baseball diamond, and Angel jabbed a pencil at me during recess. That brought us to blows after school, and neither of us was the victor. We were fools, in fact, because just as Angel caught me with a roundhouse punch to my temple that sent my head twisting to the side, out of the corner of my eye I made out Maya walking with Gilbert Romo, a guy from sixth grade who was strong enough to put us both into headlocks and trot us gently into a brick wall.

I was thinking of Angel and me, and our past. This was all we had. The past. He was *mi carnal*, the guy I hung with. I was going to miss him and our crazy ways.

Then the wind picked up, and try as I might, I couldn't anchor myself in Angel's yard. The leaves scuttled, and a tree snapped under the wind. I bounced from his yard westward toward downtown. The leaves were releasing themselves in their simple deaths, and, I suppose, I should have been doing the same.

CHAPTER
Three

THE WIND deposited me downtown and then
weakened to nothing more than a draft. I anchored myself on the Fulton Mall by tightening
my stomach and willing myself not to blow away
like litter. I meandered among its stores, all Mexican
or Hmong-owned, and none of them doing good
business at that early hour. The sun rode over a tall
building. The few city pigeons and sparrows re-
sponded to the bright but cold sun by warbling and
chirping. These birds were a natural sanitation crew;
they pecked at popcorn and the shells of sunflower
seeds. They hauled away hot dogs, burger buns,
doughnuts, *churros,* and other food that messy shoppers tossed as they went from one store window to
the next. What the shoppers were buying was anyone's guess.

I'm dead, I thought as I turned and scanned the sights of one sad, ugly mall. I ain't a part of this no more. I ain't a part of a family, either, just a word on my parents' lips—Chuy, Chuy, Chuy. I was a sad chant one day after I got killed.

I shrugged. I hitched up my pants and entered a boutique that sold candles, ceramic pots, and plastic flower arrangements. The salesclerk was a girl that I went to elementary school with. I forgot her name and she wouldn't have remembered mine, either. She probably wouldn't even recognize me. "I got nothing to show, anyway," I laughed to myself. I was invisible and touchable as light.

"Hey, girl!" I called.

She turned a page of *People en Español.* There was more intrigue in those pages than in me, the ghost. She licked a finger and turned another page. I blew my cold breath on her and she shuddered, then got up and put on the sweater that hung on a chair, and returned to reading. The girl couldn't keep her eyes off the dudes in those pages!

"You remember me?" I asked.

She turned the page of the magazine.

Speed reader, I thought. I shrugged my shoulders and swung around to size up the place. It was sorry; business was nonexistent. Even some of the candles were drooping. The plastic flowers were faded. The ceramic pots were ready to crumble back into clay. I also noticed that there was a rack of cards—birthday, anniversary, wedding announcements. I wondered if there was a Sorry-Your-Son-Was-Stabbed Card. I would have looked except, out of the corner of my eye, I saw the dude with yellow shoes pass by in a hurry. He was dressed in the same pants but he was bundled up in a Raiders jacket that was two sizes too large. Yellow shoes and a black-and-silver jacket? The dude had no sense of color coordination, definitely no Señor GQ.

"*Cabrón,*" I hissed, my hands closing into fists. "It's you."

I flew through the glass door and bounced toward the dude. I sidled up to him—it was him all right, the one with the mean face of a teenage rat. He had sharp front teeth and narrow eyes charged with the red of spilled blood. His hair was slicked back, oily. He was exactly as I remembered, but taller and leaner, as if what he ate went right through him and down the toilet.

"You're the one!" I accused.

He kept walking.

"How come?" I asked.

He slowed to a stop in front of a *panadería* with its oven of bread smells wafting from inside. His eyes locked on the gingerbread pig cookies. His sneaky attention then wheeled to a mother and a boy, cookie in hand, coming out of the bakery. He had the look of a lowlife ready to snag the treat from the child's hand.

I frosted his neck with my breath as a sort of warning. He turned away from the mother and child and slapped his neck as if a mosquito had settled its long needle into his skin. He was confused as he walked away, a worry line on his brow.

"You can't see me, huh?" I said.

I had to laugh. I thrust my hand just left of his heart and let him feel the coldness of a ghostly fist. He staggered, weirded out by a sensation he couldn't recognize. I next stabbed my spear hand into his lower back and right above his navel, the places where he had gotten me.

"Ay," he moaned.

I began to sense my own power. I could go where I pleased, and I possessed an invisible touch that made people feel me. My killer was feeling me, though he might have thought it was the coolness of morning among the tall buildings of downtown. He shrugged his collar around his throat. He breathed out and saw his breath hang in the air, then break apart and disappear. He breathed out again and punched his frosty breath with a quick jab.

"How do you like it?" I asked. He had taken my life—or did I mean my body? After all, I still had a sense of myself and a place in this world. It was just a different reality.

He glanced over his shoulder, as if he regretted not going inside the *panadería* to feast on those pig cookies. He was aware that something was happening to him, though guilt was not part of it. He reacted instinctively. He reached for his knife in his front pocket and would have pulled it out except a pair of heavy cops with the look of the pig cookies had rounded the corner from Tulare Street. They were walking our way, not the least in a hurry, because what crime occurs in the morning? Crimes— like my death, anyone's death—always take place at night.

"How come?" I mouthed at Yellow Shoes. I plunged my hand into his pocket and touched the knife that had touched me dead.

Yellow Shoes peered down at the front of his pocket. This stopped the cops, the weirdness of a dude flapping open his jacket and looking at the area around his crotch. The cops sized him up, but almost immediately their attention was drawn away by the radio squawking on the belt of the shorter of the two cops.

"You thinking about me?" I asked. "Or them?"

While Yellow Shoes hurried away, I clung to his back like the bad memory of the night before. He started walking in a hurry, then running, and I had to laugh to myself because the *vato*, lean as he was,

was out of shape. He was huffing big time, and all because of me.

"Giddy-up, burro!" I hollered, and whipped his *nalgas* with an invisible hand.

I learned that I could cling to a person for a free ride. I stayed on his back, taking in the sights of inner-city Fresno. I passed abandoned homes, run-down stores, a sloppy game of hoop at Dickey's Playground, and car lot upon car lot of rides that were waxed shiny outside but corroded under the hood. The billboards advertised a bail bondsman and check-cashing services.

I couldn't read the burro's mind, but I sensed that he had a meeting with someone—a dude with a longer blade than the one in his pocket? He strutted with purpose. Then he uttered the words, "Fat-face Fausto."

Fausto? I had gone to middle school with a kid named Fausto. He was a year older than me, and three years dumber. He was mean as a snake, a bully who every day thrust his hands into the pockets of small kids for their lunch money. That had been his thing in elementary school and junior high, until he tried it on one short kid who speared his throat and beat his ass. The kid, a Filipino, was schooled in martial arts, and was strong and dart-fast.

Yellow Shoes took a sharp right into an alley and

dropped his blade into a Dumpster. A horde of flies was disturbed by this unexpected delivery. The flies were feasting on something dead, fruit or meat, or lapping up something sugary, like on the lid of an ice-cream carton. *Yeah, that's it,* I told myself. *Flies going to town on ice cream!*

There, in the alley, I breathed into Yellow Shoes's ear, and he cupped it with his hand. He could sense me. I frosted his other ear with the warning, "Watch your back, *ese,*" and jumped off. I was tired of the free ride. I followed him as he jogged up the alley and cut through a yard of the same apartment building where the cops had earlier set things straight— the husband and wife were on the balcony, looking down on children playing in the oil-splotched driveway. This married couple seemed tired, their dark eyes a nest of wrinkles. Two babies were clinging to their legs—the children wouldn't let go until they were sixteen or so. Their marriage was going to work out, it seemed, though there would be other broken pots and vases cracked over the husband's stubborn head. In time, he would figure it out.

Yellow Shoes leaped over a kid on a tricycle and, hoisting up pants that were nearly falling off his skinny ass, ran across the street to a house painted white on one side and green on the other—an eyesore, my *papi* would argue. Someone had started a weekend project he couldn't finish. Yellow Shoes entered the house without knocking, and I did the same by going through the wall.

The living room was jammed with bicycles, all stolen, I figured. There were cruisers and mountain bikes with mud still caked to the tires. I was surprised that Yellow Shoes hadn't tossed the kid off the tricycle and carried another stolen good into the house.

"Fausto," Yellow Shoes called.

Fausto appeared from the kitchen and was, in fact, the dude I knew from middle school. He was sporting a dingy wife-beater, and blowing on a bowl of steaming *menudo*. What was it, eight years since I had seen him thrust a hand into a little kid's pocket for money? The dude was big. His gut was a slab of fat. A front tooth was missing, and, in a way, he was missing, too. He had dropped out and dropped out of sight. So this is what he was doing. Stealing bikes and porking out?

"Where you been?" Fausto asked, then blew on his *menudo* and took a careful sip from a soupspoon.

Yellow Shoes looked down at his murderous hands. He had no answer he could toss into the air to make conversation.

"Killing," I filled in for him. "Tell him you been killing."

"How come you wearing those sissy shoes?" Fausto asked.

Yellow Shoes sucked in his cheek in anger. I could tell that he didn't like being spoken to in that voice. Also, he liked his shoes.

I approached Fausto and blew on his *menudo* for him. I put my arms around him all nice. God, I hated him in middle school and was hating him now even more. What was he but a thug who pushed people off bicycles and yelled, "It's mine now. Get your face outta here!"

"I been doing stuff," Yellow Shoes answered.

Doing stuff? I wondered. *Is that all it was?*

Fausto spooned soup into his mouth and chewed. I could tell he was surprised that his morning meal had cooled. I liked being invisible. I turned away and mounted one of the bikes, my hands on the handlebars. It was a nice ride, one that I would have liked when I was a kid.

"We got to move these by nine tomorrow," Fausto said. He pointed vaguely at the bikes in the corner, all of them with red tags. *Damn,* I thought, *Fausto's all organized.* Maybe he wasn't so dumb after all. But he was sure uglier now, with his tooth gone and his bloated belly.

"I want my money now," Yellow Shoes demanded.

"You'll get it later, Chuy."

Nah, man, I thought, *we share the same name? Qué gacho!* What rotten luck! Still, I gave him the name Yellow Shoes, not Chuy. That was my name!

Yellow Shoes made a face and demanded, "I want it now, man."

Fausto sucked up a wiggly length of *tripas* and stirred his soup with his spoon. He rolled his tongue over his remaining front teeth. "You'll get it."

Yellow Shoes spread his coat and mounted his hands on his skinny hips. *I want it now,* his stance said. He then made a brave move and spoke up. "Right now, man."

"'Right now, man,'" Fausto squeaked back. He laughed and pushed his hand under his wife-beater and rubbed his belly. A tattoo of a bikini-clad woman showed. *Qué asco!*

Yellow Shoes patted his front pocket, but then remembered that his blade was in a Dumpster, flies grubbing on my old, dried blood.

Fausto set his bowl down on a table stacked high with *Lowrider* magazines, slapped his hands clean, and said, "All right. I owe you, don't I?" He left the room, pulling up the back of his pants. They were hanging so low, they showed his *chones,* which he was wearing inside out. I could see the label—his waist was a thirty-eight.

I got off the bike. I breathed in Yellow Shoes's ear, "I'd run if I were you, *tonto.*" I had a premonition that no good was about to happen, and when I swiveled my body around, I jumped into the air at the sight of Fausto, a fat locomotive, charging out of the kitchen. I'm certain that he was done with breakfast and was ready for a little workout.

"No!" Yellow Shoes yelled, left arm raised.

But what was "no" to a dude who made his living off stolen goods? He struck Yellow Shoes in the mouth. Fausto clipped him with an uppercut to his jaw; apparently he was a face-attacker. But I was wrong! Fausto pumped a couple of good shots into Yellow Shoes's ribs, a left and a right that made me wince. I hated getting hit in the stomach because there was hardly any padding on me—even in life.

"Stop it, man!" Yellow Shoes cried. He danced behind some bicycles and they began to fall over.

"'Stop it, man!'" Fausto mimicked in a whiny voice. He had a look of pleasure on his face, like he was playing pinball.

But the early massacre stopped when Fausto's cell phone began to ring. Fausto, breathing hard, glared at Yellow Shoes, smoothed his hair, and reached into his pocket. "Yeah?" he asked. His eyes were still locked on his foe, who was desperately trying to pull off a brake cable from a bicycle to use like a whip once round two began.

I heard the voice on the other end of the phone ask, "What's happenin', dawg?"

"Nothing. Just kickin' the shit out of Chuy here." He giggled at that remark.

Then the voice became a muddle of words I

couldn't make out. Fausto wagged his head once and clicked the phone off. He examined his thumb—it was red with *menudo* broth. He sucked his thumb like a baby and burped. "Now, where was I?"

Yellow Shoes sniffled. He was holding a brake cable in his hand.

"So you think you're all bad." Fausto laughed.

"You started it, homes, not me."

"'You started it, homes,'" Fausto mimicked. He picked up his bowl of *menudo* and stirred its heavy broth with a spoon. "It's all cold, man! I can't eat my breakfast in peace." Still, he took a spoonful and ate, clicking his tongue because it was so good. The dude had no manners; eating in front of someone and not sharing.

I was tired of the show. I stepped through the wall and ventured into the street. Two dogs were sniffing each other as they went round and round, head to tail. Across the street, two kids on the front lawn were playing sword fight with rolled-up newspapers. It seemed like a lot of fun, and good practice for a time when they might need to know such a skill. Then a herd of kids appeared, all laughing, and some barefoot. They had no sense of seasonal changes, no sense that it was no longer summer but mid-fall.

"God," I mouthed, my head lifted skyward. "Are you really up there?"

The wind was picking up. My instincts were picking up, too. I could always hunt Yellow Shoes later. I had somewhere else to go. I winced when I heard a scream coming from the house. Someone was hurting, and, thank God, it wasn't me. It wasn't anyone decent, just two thugs heading for an early grave.

I WAS GOING TO say good-bye to Rachel, a girl I knew when she and I were little. She beat me up a lot, the *cholita,* and once stole my trike when I was just out of my Pampers. I knew everything about her. We grew up together on the same street. She was bad, and at thirteen had a tattoo on her arm that said *mala.* In time she wiggled into a tight dress and looked fine. But she was always tough, crazy, and a mess—her dad was in Corcoran, her mother a barfly in red shoes and a skirt too short for her age. While I don't blame her, Rachel was one of the reasons why I became a ghost. That evening I was killed, she and I were going to hook up. I liked her a lot, even when she sometimes taunted me by saying, "You remember when I used to kick your ass?" Rachel, my girl from my childhood. I would go through the pain of yet another deadly exit if it meant one long kiss from her. A swap of tongues, a tight embrace under the full moon of October. Yeah, I would do it again.

When I passed through the wall of her house, she was sitting on the couch, the TV muted. Though it was almost noon, she was dressed in her pajamas. Her eyes were red. A smudge of black mascara on her cheek was the color of twilight. I suspected at first that she had a headache, because she was rubbing her forehead. Then I saw: She was applying a face ointment, a preventive measure for pimples? She was sad about me, yet thinking about how to look pretty. It made sense, more sense than what was appearing on television: a muscle truck was crawling up the back of a Volkswagen Beetle.

I sat next to her on the couch.

"Rachel," I whispered.

She began rubbing the soft area under her eyes. A small mirror rested on her knees.

"Rachel," I called. "It's me. Your *novio* who never got home."

I had to reflect on that piece of truth. Was that really my status—a *novio*? A boyfriend? I was claiming a title I hadn't earned. We hadn't even danced together, let alone walk hand in hand at school.

She stopped fussing with her looks when I blew a coldness on her throat. When I blew on her ear, she felt a presence. She put down the jar in her hand and stood up, the mirror flashing as it fell to the floor. She touched the top button of her pajamas and buttoned it. The girl was modest.

"Rachel," I mouthed. "I never even had the chance to hold your hand."

She wet her lips with the bud of her tongue. "Oh, Chuy," she remarked absently. She was thinking of me after all.

"It didn't hurt that much," I lied, touched that she thought of me. I closed my eyes and shuddered at the pain of the knife in my lower back. That had hurt. And it hurt to watch my blood spill and pool in the corner of the restroom. I opened my eyes because I had seen enough.

Rachel crossed the living room and stood over the floor furnace. She was cold from my presence. The cuffs of her pajamas fluttered from the wavering rise of heat.

I looked down at the mirror on the floor. I couldn't see myself, only a crack in the ceiling.

"Rachel," I said in a pleading voice. I wanted her as my girl. My loneliness was deep as that mirror. What could I do but feel self-pity because the one life I had was gone?

I sat on Rachel's couch, and using all my will, I snapped off the television set. The monster truck had been climbing onto the back of a Chevy Nova Super Sport, the kind of car that I would have gotten if I had lived. The destruction disappeared in an egg of light, and the television screen went black.

Rachel put a hand to her mouth. She brought the hand from her mouth. "Chuy?"

"Yeah, it's me," I answered. I could see that she was beginning to shiver, in spite of her position over the furnace vent.

"I'm sorry, Chuy."

And she was. Tears formed in her eyes and spilled in a long line down her cheeks. I noticed that more tears were coming out of her left eye and was troubled that I couldn't ask my biology teacher, Mr. Knight, about tears, why one eye would tear more than the other. Then again, I could have asked why some people cry over romantic movies while the guys I ran with watched the screen dry-eyed, their hands buttery from the popcorn.

"Chuy, you shouldn't have gone." She rubbed her index finger under her nose. She reached into her pajama pocket for a Kleenex.

"It's okay," I said. "I'm still getting around."

Then I saw how that would soon change. My left foot was gone! It had disappeared, and this frightened me. I touched the place where my foot had been. "Man, it's gone," I whispered. I looked around the living room, as if my foot had just walked off. Maybe it's in the kitchen. Who knows? It could be walking down the street right now.

"Jesus," I moaned. "I'm dying after all." But I

realized that I was already dead, though my spirit, it seemed, was going as well. First this foot, then the other?

"Chuy," Rachel cried, her face pinched with lines. "Jesús, Jesús."

Jesús, I wondered. Was she calling for Christ, or for me, a seventeen-year-old ghost disappearing one body part at a time?

She cried over the floor furnace, and, with her face smeared with mascara, pushed away from the wall. She walked down the hallway that led to the bedrooms, but I didn't follow. I then heard water running in the bathroom. The shower went on, and it was time for me to leave the house. It was time to see my parents, two souls who were crying, maybe in front of the muted television, over the loss of a son.

CHAPTER
Four

I FELT THE NEED to say good-bye to my parents and to my uncle Richard and cousin Eddie, plus friends, distant friends, and every kind soul I had met on the street. Then there was my track coach, Mr. Morales, who was just out of Fresno State and could run faster than any of his distance runners. Maybe I could find out where he lived and run over there. Until now, I never understood what "good-bye, *adios,* see you later, alligator" meant. I always assumed that I would go to school in the morning and come back in the afternoon, and things would be the same. Now I knew different.

I left Rachel's house, disturbed because my foot was gone and because I knew that in time—three days? four days?—I would disappear. I felt lighter— the wind picked up and, like it or not, I was tossed westward again back to downtown and the Fulton Mall. I peered into the boutique that I had visited earlier, and the girl—what's her name?—was still reading *People en Español,* a different issue, but still speeding along and taking in the fashions. There were no customers; she had to find ways to kill time. I guess she could think about how to prop up those drooping candles or put a little color back in those plastic flowers.

I straddled a splintery bench and listened to the spines of water splashing from a fountain. Sparrows flew through my ribs, and a pigeon the color of cement pecked at the sidewalk. I realized that I was neither hungry nor thirsty, and that the *Mexicano* pushing a *paleta* cart didn't draw me to his tinkling bell. Two children were hacking away at plates of peanut brittle. That sweet candy didn't tease me either.

In the distance, Saint John's Cathedral's mighty clock bonged one o'clock. Its single note absorbed all the sounds in the air, and then vanished. I felt a sadness for myself, but had to grin. I suddenly remembered Rachel. I could have followed her into the shower and got an eyeful. *Chihuahua!* To watch her undo one button after another, and step out of her pajamas. *Sin vergüenza!* Still, I wagged my head and told myself, *You had your chance.*

I brooded as my thoughts swung from the image

of Rachel soaping her body to the image of my casket. I had a sense that my funeral was going to be at Saint John's, where I was baptized, had my first holy communion, and was confirmed in my *primo*'s hand-me-down suit. If I had not grown too tall, maybe I could be buried in that suit. No sense wasting money on clothes no one would see, I figured.

How many days does it take to dress the dead? I wondered. I buried my face in my hands and scrubbed my face. I wanted to wake up from this nightmare. Pitched in that darkness, I had to wonder about what follows death. Do we come back? Once you've lived, is that it? Does heaven exist? Hell with its thermostat turned all the way up? I shivered at the thought of always having to stay in a grave, your own private jail.

Enough, I told myself. *Get those images out of your head!*

I watched the few shoppers in the mall, none of them happy about what they had bought, and headed westward, my shoulders slumped. I walked painlessly through a train that was hauling new cars. Where was the train headed? Oakland? Sacramento? I considered hopping one and going and going until I was in Oregon or even Canada. But I hesitated. I followed its red light until it disappeared on the horizon.

Now that I was dead, I had to grow up. I had to

confess my first real sin. My grandfather was buried at a cemetery on East Belmont, where the vineyards and orchards started. I took long, bouncing strides toward the cemetery. My grandfather had died six years ago, of cancer they told me, though it could have been anything because what did I know? At the time, I was eleven, a *mocoso* kid who just loved to play and eat candy. I was determined to repent to my grandfather about something I had stolen. It was a cigarette lighter, which I had snagged from his pants pocket and traded for ten dollars in dimes with a kid across the street.

I located Grandfather's grave immediately because I remembered that he had been buried near a diseased tree that had been cut down. I perched myself on the tree stump and said a little prayer over his flowerless grave. His headstone read simply: MARIA JESÚS CHAVEZ, 1931–1997. A single rose was etched into its polished granite.

"Grandfather," I called. "It's me—Chuy."

A distant tree rustled an answer for him.

I swallowed.

"I stole your lighter," I confessed.

Somewhere a gardener was starting up a mower.

"I also snagged some pennies, Grandpa."

The mower stopped, but a mower in the next cemetery started up. I floated off the tree stump.

"You probably knew that I took it," I added.

I clearly remembered going through his pocket and pulling out not only his cigarette lighter but also ten pennies dark as his work-weathered skin. I remembered running outside the house and meeting up with the neighbor kid—Jonathan Something-or-other. He liked the lighter so much that he went inside and stole two rolls of dimes worth ten dollars. He stole the dimes, I think, from his dad, but he lied and said they were his. All I remember was the weight of those rolls of dimes and how slowly I peeled the paper off like they were Life Savers. I bought candy for two weeks and ate it alone in a tree in my backyard.

Grandpa, I'm the one, I confessed in my heart. *You know—the lighter, the pennies.*

I recalled how Jonathan used the lighter to start a small fire in his backyard. We were both eleven, self-ish beyond words, and guilty. How many candy bars smudged my dirty face?

"Grandpa," I whispered. "How is it down there?"

I smoothed the grass in front of his tombstone and told him that I was sorry and that I was dead and maybe I would be with him. If I could have cried hot, dime-sized tears, I would have. But what could I do but trace his name with my finger? I put my hands through his headstone and dipped my right arm all the way to my shoulder into the moist lawn. This scared me. I thought that I might touch his bony chest, shredded to almost nothing from years and years of rain.

"Ah, Grandpa," I sobbed. I could swear that I felt his hand tugging mine. Was Grandpa trying to bring me down?

I noticed at the next grave a bee trying to suck on an artificial flower. It seemed real, the flower. I floated over to an open grave. It was dark, and a few roots showed from the sides of the wall. I jumped into the grave and looked skyward, wondering if this is what the dead see for eternity. A bird flew past, then another.

"I'm sorry, Grandpa," I whispered. Dirt from the sides of the grave crumbled.

From the graveyard, I returned to town, pushing hard because the wind was blowing against my steps. It was getting dark. Some headlights of passing cars were on. And it was by this light that I noticed my other foot was gone, and a portion of my left hand, the one I had used to trace Grandfather's name.

Nah, I thought. I held up my hand as if it were something foreign to me.

I tightened my stomach and forced myself to continue. Wind or no wind, I was going to see my parents.

MOM AND DAD weren't home, though the living room and hallway lights were burning brightly. Were they leaving the lights on for me? Did they leave a plate of cookies and milk on the kitchen table? I went into the kitchen. Our cat, Samba, was cleaning herself on the table. If my mom had seen her, she would have glared at that ignorant cat and chased her from the house with an open palm. Samba gazed at me, her back leg in the air. The cat sensed me, and stood up, arched her back, and jumped off the table. She went over to her water bowl, but just stared.

Where were Mom and Dad? I wondered.

They were probably at *mi abuela*'s house, breaking the news of my death not once but two or three times. Grandma was hard of hearing, even when she was hearing well! She was stubborn, just like my mom, and wouldn't listen, in either Spanish or English, to anyone if it was something she didn't want to hear. Poor Grandma was a mother of three sons. Two were already dead from the same car accident. These two sons—the uncles I hardly knew, except by their Christmas presents—had been returning home from a fishing trip in the Sierras and their car just went off the road. No explanation, no theory even. The car, the sheriffs wrote, plunged down a ravine.

The telephone started to ring and I watched it for fourteen rings until it stopped. Who was calling? Who was curious about my death, or should I say *murder*? Until then, it hadn't really occurred to me that I had been murdered. But three stab wounds in three places? What else could you call it?

I sat on the couch in the living room, then stood up with a jerk. I would have cried if I'd had tears inside me. Mom had brought out a dusty photo album. She had it turned to a page of pictures from when I was about eight. In one, I was sitting on Grandpa's rickety lap.

"No," I whispered.

In the photo, Grandpa's cigarette lighter was on the coffee table. Grandpa was caught off guard; his eyes were half closed. And me? I was looking at the lighter, not at the camera, and I could tell by my devilish eyes that I wanted badly to possess it. I had the look of greed.

"You were so bad," I muttered, shaking my head.

There were other photos of me at Disneyland. My face was all orange and my teeth, it seemed, were really huge in my face. I then spied the news clippings of my murder. There were three of them— one from our newspaper and the others, I suspected, brought over by family and friends of the family. The news clippings were already ragged.

Samba pranced into the living room and leaped onto the coffee table. I petted her with an invisible hand. I tickled her chin. When I blew my cold breath on her collar, she jumped away and hurried back into the kitchen.

I heard a car pull up in the driveway, and the living room brightened from the headlights that cut through the heavy curtains.

"They're home," I said to myself.

I brought my hands to my face. I cringed at having to observe my mother and father with their faces wet from the deep sorrow of their only son's death. I had seen Mom cry maybe three or four times, and my dad once. But that was when the Raiders had lost a playoff game that would have sent them to the Super Bowl. Dad was a funny dude. Crying over a football game! Maybe now I would see him crying a second time.

The key worked in the lock of the front door, and the door pushed open. My parents, followed by Uncle Richard and my mom's *comadre*, Carmen, entered with their faces lowered. They were ghosts themselves, white in spite of their Mexican-ness. They had stopped crying, but their eyes were red. Then others came in, some of them family, and a guy who worked with Dad. My *primo* Eddie followed, brushing his feet against the carpet. His eyes were red, too.

When the telephone began to ring, they all turned their heads. My mom pushed past Uncle Richard.

Nah, Mom, I thought. *It's not me.*

She answered the telephone. She listened, but

didn't say anything until she hung up and then said to the crowd, to no one, really: "Mary's making a cake."

A cake for my funeral?

After I was buried, they were going to have a little gathering. There would be more than a cake, I realized, and a lot more crying than what was going on now. Carmen was dabbing her nose with a Kleenex. Carmen was always dabbing her nose with a Kleenex; her life's complaint was something about always having a cold. Maybe she had one now. Then again, she could be crying for my mom and dad, and me.

Uncle Richard went into and returned from my bedroom. He was holding up a couple of cross-country ribbons. All of them were second or third place. I was never good at track, just some lanky kid who ran for the fun of it. If I medalled, great. If I didn't, *pues,* I could at least get a T-shirt and a squeeze bottle for my Gatorade.

"Are these the ones?" Uncle Richard asked. He held up the ribbons like nooses.

My dad nodded his head.

The two examined the ribbons. Where was the neck that they hung from? Where was the body that brought them home?

"I can get them mounted." Uncle Richard rubbed the faces of the coin-shaped medals, and I wiped my forearm against my eyes. But no tears would spring up. I broke away from the two of them and went into the kitchen, where someone had plugged in the coffeepot. The brown liquid was slowly filling up the pot.

I can't believe it, I thought. I hadn't even lived long enough to drink coffee.

Then Mom appeared, pulling anxiously on Eddie's sleeve. Mom's tears were gone, and replaced by angry fire. It was the look she had on her face whenever I was bad and she'd step quickly into the bedroom for Dad's belt.

"I want you to do it!" she snapped.

Eddie looked away.

"Come on, *mi'jo,* you can do it."

Do what? I wondered.

"I can't—it's wrong," Eddie answered. He flapped his arms at his side.

My mom let her eyes fill with tears. She pouted and produced lines around her nose.

"It won't solve anything," Eddie explained vaguely, looking up and challenging Mom with a hard gaze.

When the first tear rolled down her cheek, Eddie turned and left the kitchen by the back door. Mom, sniffling, glared at the coffeepot as if she hated it for not brewing fast enough. She brought out a coffee cup and, strangely, a single tear fell into the cup. Coffee and tears, plus a single spoonful of sugar. It was going to be one of those evenings. I had to get out of there.

IT HAD BEEN an embarrassing year for football at our high school. By late October, we were 2–5 in our conference. Everyone, including our players—who hid their shame behind face masks—joked that our two wins came because the other team hadn't shown up. Luckily, basketball season was kicking in, and I was friends with some guys on the team—Jamal Baines, Jaime Rodriguez, Jonathan Koo, and Jared Mitchell. The four Js, I called them, and they called me Mr. Lean because I was a distance runner. There was not a pinch of baby fat on my body. God, if they could see me now! I was so skinny that you couldn't see me anymore!

On the court, my homie friends were fair, at best, and none of them was a starter. We were supposed to be good this year, or at least look *suave* because we had new uniforms. Maybe new jockstraps, too!

It was Saturday evening, and I knew that we would be playing an exhibition game against Sanger High. From my parents' home I strode, bounced, and flowed toward the high school. This took some effort because the wind worked against me. I almost gave up when I noticed my hands were gone, and one of my ankles, too. I was being erased right before my eyes!

"No," I murmured.

Unable to continue, I had to sit on a curb and bury my face in my arms. I tried not to picture my mom and dad, who in my mind were staring into their cups of coffee for an answer to my death. I was so mad at Yellow Shoes. I possessed the sudden urge to hurt him.

"How come me?" I cried. I knew some crackheads who needed to go. But why me? What trouble did I cause people? After a few minutes, I pulled myself together and continued toward school. I would see what I would miss—the start of basketball season.

Since it was an exhibition game, there weren't many spectators in the bleachers. There were cheerleaders and the band, and Coach Silva dressed in a black suit. He wasn't a bad guy, really, except I held it against him when he cut me off the squad. I wasn't tall enough. I couldn't make a layup, even with no pressure. So? I wanted badly to be with my friends, the four Js. I recalled how Coach pulled me aside and said, "Hey, track season's in two months, no?"

I scanned the bleachers. I recognized some of my classmates. I saw Jamal, Jaime, Jonathan, and Jared huddled around Coach. What would these dudes do except sit and chew their fingernails when the game began? I liked them a lot and was beginning to think of using the word *love*. Yeah, I loved my friends, whose eyes, I noticed, were red from crying. The skin under their eyes was dark. No doubt they had been up all night talking about me as they drove around Fresno, killing time.

Then I spotted a banner with my name on it. There were flowers pinned to the banner, and a lot of signatures and drawn hearts. Did people really like me? I wasn't exactly popular; then again, I wasn't exactly one of those nerdy souls that hug the hallways, looking down at their shoes as they shuffle from class to class. But flowers and hearts?

The clock read ten minutes before game time. Time was running out and, with it, my time on this planet, in this gym that was bright as a carnival.

I searched the meager crowd for Rachel, my would-be *novia*. But she wasn't the kind of person who went to football or basketball games. I looked for another girl that I liked, but she wasn't there, either. But there was my history teacher, Miss Escobedo, whom I'd had a crush on since I first saw her get out of her car in a short dress. Hers was the only class I really liked; that one and maybe English and lunch. Miss Escobedo was only twenty-five or so, and sweet.

"Dawg," I whined.

Miss Escobedo had her arm hooked in some guy's arm.

I sat in the bleachers next to Sara, a girl who had tried out for cheerleading. Like me with basketball, she didn't make it. But she was nice and had a nice smile, and used the word *nice* a lot when she talked. I got up when a friend of hers returned with a bag of popcorn.

"That's nice of you," Sara said, her face lit with happiness over the prospect of eating popcorn through the first half.

Her friend, too, had gone out for cheerleading. But she hadn't made it either.

"It's nice to see you," I breathed in Sara's ear.

Sara touched her ear.

"You can't do everything," I said, and left her side. I approached the vice principal, Mr. Laird. He was holding a clipboard and clicking his pen nervously. I would have reached over and touched the pen to make him stop, but my hands were long gone.

Coach Silva turned to Mr. Laird. He nodded his head.

Mr. Laird stood up, breathed in, and clicked the on-and-off switch of a handheld microphone.

"School," he began.

That single word echoed off the walls. Everyone grew quiet, even the visiting team. The mood became dark, as they were aware of what was going to be announced.

"School," he repeated. "Yesterday we lost one of our students in an unfortunate incident. It troubles me."

Mr. Laird did look troubled, looked like someone who had swallowed a dark cloud. I had always thought he was mean, but I could see that I had been wrong. His lower lip quivered as he held back from actually crying. I would have hated to have his job right then. A grown man crying in front of his school.

"May we have a minute of silence?" he asked. He scanned the gymnasium until everyone's head was bowed.

A kid I'd known since elementary school stood up, raising a trumpet to his mouth. I couldn't remember his name, but couldn't forget how a bully used to jack him up for his lunch money. And every day this kid—this trumpet player with thick glasses and more than his share of pimples—would bring out his money before the bully even asked. Now, years later, he was playing taps for me.

"Ah, man," I sobbed. When was the crying going to stop?

The kid from my childhood played beautifully. I felt terrible that I couldn't go back in time and try to beat up the bully for him. We could have done it together.

After the trumpet player lowered his trumpet, a last note hung in the air. Mr. Laird asked for silence and a moment of prayer. But I already knew silence. It occurred earlier when I stood before an open grave looking up at the October sky in midday.

Then the game started with an easy bucket for Sanger. That basket was followed by two more. With less than three minutes gone, Sanger was up 6–0.

Sapo *luck,* I complained silently as I remained an invisible spectator in the bleachers. I screamed: "Come on, dawgs—score!"

CHAPTER
Five

YELLOW SHOES. After I left the basketball game, I found *another* dude in a set of yellow shoes hanging in front of a 7-Eleven. He was sucking the last of a cherry-flavored slush. His cheeks collapsed as he inhaled that sweet, meaningless drink. His eyes were roving in their sockets as he scrutinized the oil-stained parking lot. Let him blame society, school, and his deadbeat father. He could care less. He was trouble. His face was half-light, half-dark, under the glare of a sputtering neon sign. It was the dark side of his face that attracted me.

"Who are you?" I asked, face-to-face, as if we were two boxers right before the start of a fight. "How come you got the same stupid shoes on?"

It was trippy encountering another *vato* in yellow

shoes. I wondered if that was the new style for gang bangers. But unlike the skinny guy who did me, this dude in front of the store was heavy as a sack of onions, fat and out of breath just sucking in his drink. He tossed his cup, looked left and right, and hiked up his loose and *huango* Dickies cut off at the knees. He approached a Honda with different-colored fenders and a spiderweb of a cracked windshield. The fat dude disappeared into the shadows and his hand wiggled the passenger's window, which was open an inch. The inch was enough for him to work his wormy fingers inside. He wiggled the window back and forth until it, too, cracked and cobwebbed. With both hands, he bent the window and unlatched the door.

"Ay," he yapped. A finger, nipped by a sliver of glass, went into his mouth like a candy cane. He shook his finger and muttered, "Stupid glass."

This ride didn't have an alarm and barely any tread on the tires—they were shiny as a bald man's head. The fenders could fall off hitting a pothole. This was the kind of car that got you from one place to another in truly ugly style. It was a car even Hmong and Mexican gangs wouldn't consider stealing. Nasty junior high kids wouldn't bother to bend the antenna. The junk man would laugh, run a hand-kerchief under his nose, and laugh some more. As for organizations that search for donated cars? One look and they would drive away. The Honda was on its way to becoming scrap metal.

Maybe this dude was practicing the art of thievery. Maybe he couldn't help himself. He opened the door, and jumped in quickly, the springs squeaking under his weight. He rifled through the glove compartment and found a can of hairspray and two Bibles, *nada más*. He growled and fanned the pages of a Bible as if he were trying to cool himself. When he tossed it over his shoulder, he heard a whimper that startled him. He turned around and discovered a poodle.

"Stupid dog," he snarled. "You scared me, stupid."

Stupid, it seemed, was the main word in this *vato*'s vocabulary.

The poodle whimpered. The little furry dude, all old with black muck running from its eyes, was the one who was scared.

When the dude reached to grab the dog around the throat, I shoved the stumps of my ghostly arms into his eyes. He backed off, rubbing his peepholes, and farted the winds of fear. He farted a second time, and I laughed, *"Fuchi!"* His hand reached for the door handle.

My power is the coldness of death. I'm invisible, yet present, and this bully was comprehending my power. I had no hands, and my feet were gone. But I could make people feel my presence. This is what I was learning about myself.

The guy scrambled out of the car and hurried away, one hand pulling up his pants as he let out another fart. I would have followed him for the fun of it, but I had had enough of his ugly face. Plus, I couldn't hold my place. The wind had picked up, and I was sent rolling like a tumbleweed. Luckily for me, it was in direction of *primo* Eddie's duplex apartment, a mile or so away, in the part of town where Fausto, the bike thief, held court in his half-painted house. I rolled past the high school, where one of the teams was making a basket. *Let it be us,* I prayed. *Just this night, let us be winners.*

The wind's push eased and I was able to stand upright on a dark street—kids had busted out the streetlights for the fun and the danger of it.

I got my bearings, and ignored a car alarm that was screaming. But no one stepped out of their houses to see. What was a car alarm when better action was taking place on TV?

I recognized my *primo*'s apartment and prayed that he had left my parents' place and was home by now—what had he and my mom been talking about, anyhow? Lights were on. A radio was singing to itself, because when I went through the wall there was no one home.

Still, I called out, *"Primo?* Eddie?"

A moth banged against the bulb of the goose-necked lamp. The refrigerator kicked on, chilling the cold water even colder. I stood in the living room and was not in the least scared when a tree in the yard whistled its haunting tune.

I got comfy on the couch, my weight not even denting the cushion an inch. I noticed that both my ankles were gone, and some of my wrists. I felt a shiver blossom in my shoulders and wanted to cry. Instead, I lay on the couch and assembled in my mind something to smile about, something to remember from my crazy life. I giggled. I pictured Eddie and me crouching like frogs and playing with matches. Bad boys for a day, we were in an old lady's junky backyard, and Eddie, the brave one because he was seven and I was six, struck a couple of wooden matches at once. He cried, *"Ay!"* and tossed them over his head when the flame licked his fingertips. One match flared and caught the dry grass that was not lawn but something yellow as hay. We jumped up like frogs. I remember asking him, "Are we going to burn?" When Eddie bugged out his eyes, I knew we were in trouble. He was scared as me. We jumped and danced on the flames, but they spurted out under our little tennis shoes. The fire's great hunger began to feast on the quickly blackening grass.

I had to smile to myself as I remembered the two of us trying to climb the chain-link fence. *Trying* is the word. I got my pants cuffs caught on the top of the fence and flipped back to hang upside down, mouth open. It was weird. Out of the corner of my eye, I could see the flames grazing on the grass and the smoke begin to rise in puffs that signaled trouble. But I didn't become scared until I heard the distant wail of fire engines. I pictured the firemen with hoses and ladders. I pictured smoke curling around my body on the fence, like a chicken on a barbecue grill.

Eddie tried to unhook me, but he wasn't strong enough to lift me up and free my pants cuffs. He said that I was going to be okay, and gently let me fall back and rest against the chain-link. He ran away promising to get help. I was really scared then. I envisioned my mom burning my legs with a good belt-whipping. Now there was fire!

"Eddie, you funny dude," I said, then laughed. We were troublemaking *mocosos* that day!

It took a fireman to unhook me from the fence. I couldn't tell if he was smiling, or frowning—I was hanging upside down and couldn't tell up from down, but was smart enough to hurry away once my dizziness disappeared.

What was that—twelve years ago? Eddie was now studying air-conditioning at City College, and I was dead and losing myself to the eventual dark hallway of a wet grave.

I was looking at the wall where a slightly curled Raiders calendar was nailed when a key rattled in the door. The doorknob turned, and Eddie entered cautiously as he scanned the living room—in this part of town, there was every chance of encountering a thug waiting in the shadows. His eyes were red, his face as gray as ash. It took him a lot of effort to get the key out of the door.

He checked out the kitchen before hurrying to the bathroom to take a leak that lasted longer than I could hold my breath—if I had had breath. He didn't flush but came out zipping up. He was starting again for the kitchen when he heard a tap on the front door. Eddie froze. His eyes spun crazily in their sockets, and I sensed he was thinking about what to pick up—the coat hanger on the kitchen table, the hammer on the chair? He was searching for a weapon to use to defend himself. Who was knocking on his door at that late hour? Not some religious group asking if he wanted to be saved.

The tap came again, this time softer.

Eddie stepped toward the door and hesitated, his breathing shallow. He took a step backward and picked the hammer up off the chair. What was he going to do? Nail the intruder to the wall?

I floated over to Eddie and stood so close I could

see the pulse in his throat. He swallowed his fear and reached for the doorknob. He pulled the door open slowly. No one was there.

Light footsteps—a woman in pumps?—clicked down the driveway of the duplex. When they faded, Eddie, hammer raised, stepped outside and discovered on the mat a folded dish towel that I recognized from home—what was it doing there? When he picked it up and opened it, he found a gun, heavy as the hammer in his hand.

"Jesus," he muttered. He walked down the porch and hurried out into the driveway. *"Tía, I can't do it."*

Tía? My mother? Had Mom delivered a handgun in a towel to her nephew? It was so clear, just like the moon tangled in the nearly leafless sycamore trees. My mom expected revenge, and she chose Eddie to see to this revenge. I thought she would have known better. After all, she was a grown-up. After all, she went to church every Sunday, and didn't the Bible say something about not taking another person's life?

"Mom," I said, "you can't do this." I flapped my arms at my side, as if I, the fallen angel, could take off and leave this place. So that's what they were talking about in the kitchen.

Her old Buick's headlights lit up the black asphalt lining the street. She pulled away from the curb, and I tried to run after her with my long strides. I might have kept up with her car—she was a slow driver

/ho went by the rules and used both hands on the
steering wheel—except the wind pushed me in the
other direction.

"No!" I screamed at Mom. "You can't ask him to
do this!"

I slowed to a walk and turned around, head
down. I loved my cousin, who many years ago tried
to unhook me when I was hanging upside down. I
would crave his friendship until my body disappeared altogether. Friendship is what I longed for,
but nature was telling me to move on. When I
looked up, my cousin was setting the hammer on
top of the handgun, the tools of a terrible trade.

THE WIND that whips through the valley in fall sent
me rushing toward Blackstone Avenue then shifted
so that I once again ended up on Fausto's street. Radios were crying out Mexican songs, and over that I
heard the frying of something delicious—chicken
tacos? *Carne asada? Chicharrones?* I was aware that I
couldn't eat, but the aroma . . .

I stood in the middle of the street—and jumped
out of the street and nearly out of my mind when I
saw a ghostly outline of a girl roll past. I guessed it
right away: She was dead, like me, and recently dead
because she couldn't control her body. She was tumbling, and her long brownish hair was waving like
seaweed. Her mouth was shaped into a sorrowful O.

"Dawg," I crowed to myself.

I wasn't the only one departing life in Fresno; others were shutting their eyes as the pulse in their wrists slowed to a stop, though their watches continued to bang out the time. I felt self-centered, me thinking all along that I was the only person to have lost his life. I asked myself: *Where are the others, the old and sick who gave up their ghosts daily, or those who died in accidents? Where were those who died from cancer, heart attacks brought on by heartbreak, or diseases I couldn't even pronounce?*

This girl, I asked myself. *Who is she?*

I put my long-distance runner years to use and caught up to her just as she righted herself and wobbled dizzily. I was familiar with that sensation of dizziness, that and a lot more. Immediately, she began to style her hair back into place. Funny how she was primping even when she was a ghost. Who was there to see her but me? The sorrowful O of her mouth completely disappeared and was replaced by the sleepy look of someone shaken awake.

"You got to tighten your stomach muscles," I tried to explain.

She jumped backward, shocked by my presence. Her arms were raised in self-defense.

"Don't be scared," I said in a slow, deliberate manner. I wanted to be understood, trusted.

A curious look sprang up on her face. A line cut

across her brow, and I could see by that single little line what she would look like when she got older. Then I realized that she would never get older.

"The wind," I said. "It'll blow you around. You have to tighten your stomach muscles, get really low if you want to stay in one place." I considered raising the front of my shirt to show her how to tighten those stomach muscles, but I was afraid that she would grimace at my knife wounds.

"Who are you?" she asked.

"Chuy," I answered. I hesitated, but went ahead and boldly asked: "How did it happen? How did you die?"

She shrugged her shoulders and turned her face away. She didn't want to tell me.

But I was sure that her death had not been violent. She didn't suffer through a car wreck or a gunshot. She was whole and—I had to gulp—beautiful. Her face had the shape of a valentine heart. *You little wimp,* I scolded myself, *are you falling in love or what?* Truth is, that's how I am, or *was.* I was known for falling in love at the sight of both good-looking and not-so-good-looking girls. I wasn't very choosy. Once, when I was ten or so, I fell in love with a track star on the back of a Wheaties cereal box. She was my dream girl. I even cut her out and taped her to my bedroom wall.

"My name is Chuy," I said again. I was suddenly

embarrassed because I had no visible hands, and my feet were gone. However, she didn't appear frightened.

"Mine's Crystal," she said, then asked, "Did you hear me? Crystal, my name is Crystal."

"Yeah, I heard," I said. "I understand." It appeared that we ghosts could talk to each other.

We stood in the middle of the street, shy as ponies. When a car turned down the corner and headed our way, weaving because the driver was drunk on whatever, Crystal hurried to the sidewalk. But I stood my ground, chest slightly pushed out, in fact, and let the car go through me like I was fog. Yeah, I was showing off. I admit it, me all *macho* as I stuck out my chest at the approaching headlights. But I also wanted to show her what we ghosts could do. The whole world could smash through us and nothing would happen. A jet could fall on our heads and we would just walk away singing "Cielito Lindo."

"You're not hurt?" Crystal asked as she approached me.

Hurt? Me? I had already seen the worst in my life. A car traveling through me was painless.

"Nah," I said.

Show-off me! I leaped into the lower branches of a tree. Crystal, giggling, bent her knees and shot upward and past the tree. She smiled, formed the word "oops" on her lips, and slowly descended, holding her dress to her sides so that it didn't parachute out and reveal what was underneath. Devilish me, I considered taking a peek up her dress, but I liked her too much. Why be like that?

In the tree, her legs swinging, she told me that she was from Selma, a town outside of Fresno. I had once picked grapes there—my dad wanted me to know what it meant to labor under the sun surrounded by the wasps that buzzed through the vines. She was seventeen, a senior in high school, and vice president of the school. She was even a cheerleader.

Dang, I thought. *Vice president of a high school! A cheerleader!*

"What about you?" she asked

I couldn't say that I was cheerleader. But I could have easily been elected vice president of the lonely boys on campus. I told her that I was in high school, too. I told her that I ran track. I swallowed before I lied about the blue ribbons hung on my bedpost at home.

She gave me a squint as if she didn't believe me.

I shrugged my shoulders and giggled into my arm. I confessed that I wasn't that good at long-distance running, that I ran because it was something to do and was the only sport that I could letter in. I was too small for football and basketball. And wrestling? I had a gap-toothed girl cousin who once pinned me in seventeen seconds.

"I run track, too," Crystal said.

"No way," I argued. "You can't do everything!"

She nodded her head. "I'm good," she declared. She wasn't bragging but telling me how it was.

Mouth open, she gazed openly at where my hands should have been.

"They're gone," I said. "So are my feet."

"We're dead, huh?" she asked innocently.

"Yeah," I answered. This was weird. The two of us talking about being dead and neither of us caring, really.

"Are we going to be like this?" she asked.

I knew what she meant. She meant whether we were going to be ghosts for a long time or—she was inspecting the stumps of my arms—or if we were just going to vanish.

"I don't know," I lied. How could I tell her right away that we were slowly going to disappear?

"You're not telling me the truth!" She smiled at me because I was such a bad liar.

I shrugged my shoulders. I had no answer about what happens to us. But if she had asked me if I had liked her, I would have stuttered, "Baby, I'm for real." Or some other silly come-on line.

In turn, I was sure that she liked me, a little bit at

least. But what good was this now? Beyond her I could see the night sky and the stars giving off their icy energy. I felt like crying. How could I explain to her that I was disappearing, and that it was going to happen to her? I figured that she had died that evening, and by tomorrow, midday, maybe later, her hands would be gone along with the feet that brought her all those first-place ribbons in track. That is, if she was telling the truth and ran track. I had heard that the girl runners of Selma were better than good—great, as our coach hollered at our sorry-ass team.

"Yeah, I'm disappearing," I admitted, with a shrug of my shoulders. "It's just the way it is."

Her eyes lost their innocent luster. She frowned and examined her own hands. She was wondering whether she was going to disappear in time.

"It just happens," I explained lamely. My sorrow for myself and Crystal was as deep as any river. We were ghosts, and what happened later when we lost our ghostly bodies was a big mystery.

I told her how I had been killed at a nightclub all because I stupidly commented that I liked this guy's shoes. The shoes were yellow, really different. I told her that he killed me with a knife and lied when I said it hardly hurt at all. I bit my lower lip and hesitated about asking again how she had died.

Crystal pulled her hair behind her ear. She jumped down from the branch, and I got a sense that she didn't want to discuss her death. There was something she didn't want to share.

I jumped down, too. "Follow me," I said.

I took long strides, and she followed, almost skipping. She liked how her hair lifted, and how she could stay in the air churning her legs. She was feeling beautiful, I'm sure, and looked beautiful at that hour of night when barking dogs had shut up and were bedding down on army blankets. When the wind pushed against us, I told her to tighten her stomach muscles.

She rubbed her stomach, giggling. She blew off course for a second, actually flew up to tree level, but soon descended.

"Tighten up," she sang as she remembered what I had explained about anchoring yourself against the wind. "I got to tighten up." She laughed with a hand over her mouth, and I liked that gesture a lot. I could tell that she wasn't scared of being a ghost.

I led her down the street and in the direction of Fausto's house. I wanted to see if I could do something about his bike-stealing scam.

The lights inside his house were off.

Crystal made a face that revealed her snobbery. She didn't like the neighborhood, with its junky cars and houses leaning crookedly on their foundations. The apartment buildings were hideous. Laundry the color of defeated nations hung on lines. The screens on the windows were torn.

"It ain't that bad here," I said, though I had to admit the neighborhood was dilapidated. I climbed the steps and walked through the wall and then back out.

Wow, Crystal said through her expression. Her snobbery disappeared.

I held up the stump of my arm, beckoning her to follow.

She floated up the steps and, by my side, entered the den of nickel-and-dime thieves.

CHAPTER
Six

Fausto wasn't home, and neither was my punk killer in yellow shoes. I could live without either of them, and so could all of Fresno. Truth is, I had the suspicion that Fausto didn't really live in there, but considered the run-down place a warehouse for the stuff he ripped off. Perfect—an export business that would leave the neighborhood children crying. I could change that.

I had learned a thing or two about my body. When I touched the hinges of the front door with the stubs of my arms, the coldness of death made the hinges snap. I was providing the bikes with an escape route, though I knew they were not going to start pedaling on their own. *¡Imposible!* But I was acquainted with run-down neighborhoods. When a door was open, the street kids, spitting sunflower seed shells, would climb the steps and holler, "Hey!" maybe three times. If there was no answer, they would enter like bugs, antennas tuned to the sound of someone home. But unlike ants that carry away crumbs, these kids, praying to the Saint of Breaking and Entering, would tiptoe in like ninjas and take what pleased them.

Straddling a lowrider bicycle, Crystal watched me freeze the hinges. Together we breathed on the door until it collapsed at an angle—what was death but a cold wind, after all? She watched while biting the ends of her hair and clapped as the door fell when a draft pushed against it. The things that go knock in the night went unnoticed in this *barrio*. Not even the dogs barked.

The clock on the wall read 2:45. We were wide awake in the heart of the night. The moon had already carried itself westward and, in time, the night would shed its darkness. By five o'clock the eastern horizon would be rubbed with the pink of a new day. Fausto, a night thief, would not return until the afternoon. Or maybe not at all. He could be sleeping with some *chica* who didn't know better.

"Let's go," I told Crystal.

Crystal got off the bicycle and approached me. She grimaced at me as if I didn't make any sense. "What do you mean?"

"I have to go home," I said. Jokingly, I asked, "You want to meet my mom?"

The words *home* and *mom* had the strands of hair falling from her mouth. As we left the house and bounced down the front steps, I recognized the longing inside her. She wanted to go home herself and to say good-bye to her parents.

Still, I asked, "What are you thinking?"

"Nothing," she answered.

Nothing? The way I figured, the mind was always swirling one thought or another. It was impossible not to think something, even in sleep. But in sleep they called your thoughts dreams—or nightmares.

"Come on," I begged as I drew close to her. "Tell me."

Crystal was unafraid of the stumps of my arms. She gripped them and murmured something about disappointing her parents. About what, though? I examined her face for a clue, but found none. "What are you thinking?" I probed.

"Just something," she answered. She nervously undid the top button of her blouse.

I was aware that she was picturing her family, mom and dad, and maybe her bedroom, and her brothers and sisters, if she had any. That was what I had pictured on the roof of Club Estrella— home with Mom and Dad in front of the television.

I gritted my teeth as I remembered something else. *Dawg,* I thought. I kept a three-pack of condoms under my mattress, and none of them ever got used! In a week or so, my mom would come in and straighten up my bed and discover that box. I could see her rattling it against her ear, then start crying as she realizes that she would never have grandchildren.

Crystal lowered her face. Her beauty had me pressing my body to hers. I hugged her, and she hugged me back. Her face rested against my neck. God, how come I hadn't met her when I was living?

"I need to go back home," she said, and pushed me away gently. Her eyes had a sorrowful look that spread to me. I felt my own sorrow, which deepened when I saw that my calves were vanishing. For me, time was running out.

She moved away from me and stood in the street. She faced south toward Selma, and I could tell that she had much to say to her parents. But she didn't have the words to tell them. She was dead and a ghost, and her parents, for all I knew, were unaware of her death. She had been dead only a few hours. Perhaps her body hadn't been found yet.

Crystal, I beckoned with my eyes. Boldly, I asked, "How did you die?"

"Pills," she answered, after she searched my face for trust. I suppose she found it in my eyes. She bit her lower lip and punished it really hard because when she let go I could see the teeth marks in her lip.

Wind whipped around her, and her long hair flowed. Her skirt also flapped like wings.

A dude, I figured. A dude was involved. Why else would she kill herself? I pried and asked, "What was his name?"

She turned and started walking up the street. She intended to get back home.

I was torn whether to go back to my family or go with Crystal. She began running without a good-bye. Pitifully, I swallowed my loneliness. I couldn't stand losing her, and, nearly crying because I wasn't sure if I would be able to make it back to Fresno before disappearing altogether, I chased after her.

"Crystal," I yelled, and joked, "Let's do breakfast in Selma!" The town had no more than ten thousand people, and maybe two thousand cows and an equal number of chickens and pigs. In fact, in Selma there was every chance that your best friend was a fly-speckled pig that you fed daily from a dented pail.

I was soon running at her side, me, a perennial third-place long-distance runner. We galloped in time, left leg and then right, twin gazelles leaping in the darkness of night. I was keeping up, stride for stride, and observing the quiet street where I imagined poor families sawing logs of sleep. I imagined the warm beds and the blankets rising on each snore. I imagined a mother stumbling from bed as her baby began to kick and cry.

Crystal smiled at me, and I had to smile, though there was no happiness in my heart. I was no longer thinking of myself but of Crystal—her body lay somewhere in Fresno, maybe unclaimed because it had yet to be discovered. Right then, I poked her shoulder with the stump of my arm and got her to slow to a walk.

"Crystal," I said. "I've got to ask something."

She pulled her hair from her eyes, which were luminous in the night.

"Where did you die?"

"Don't ask," she whimpered. When her eyes narrowed, some of their brightness disappeared.

"I got to," I answered. I had to know whether her body was found, or if some stray dog was circling it. She could be in a ditch, the passenger side of a parked car, or half-clothed in a shallow grave. She was dead, I realized, but I wanted to protect her body. Maybe I could be the first to show my respect, like I'd seen on TV. People will put teddy bears, flowers, and balloons where a friend got killed.

"Why?" she asked, rocking on her heels because I was close enough to kiss her. I thought of making that kind of move, but my question was serious. Just where was she—her body? We stood like that, eyes level on each other's. Just then a car turned onto the street and both of us watched it approach, picking up speed. Crystal took my arm, squeezed her eyes shut, and we let the car pass through us.

"That's a funny feeling," she commented as she turned and watched the car continue down the street, its brake lights a sinful red as the car turned another corner. The tires squealed, but just barely.

I continued to probe. "Come on, girl, where?" I repeated. "Where did it happen?"

She pointed vaguely. "In my car."

"And where's your car?" I had to brace myself because the wind was picking up. Crystal, however, a new ghost, blew halfway down the street. I flew to her and asked again.

"At Roeding Park," she confided. She faced southward, her hair blowing and her skirt flapping, revealing thighs that were muscled from running.

Of course, I knew the park. Teenagers like us shared our loneliness in that park, where at night peacocks howled like witches. I had been one of those teenagers, me and my *carnal* Angel, both of us sitting on top of benches as we took turns complaining about life, which, for us, was mainly school, maybe parents if they were jacking us up about our laziness. I recalled the rush of wind through the eucalyptus and how that mighty tree dropped leaves.

We tore those leaves like movie tickets, leaf after leaf that kept our hands busy. We went there to talk about school and about our parents and how they didn't know us because they were always working. What was Dad anyhow except a man who worked and came home to watch television? And Mom? A gossiper whose mouth was a bud of lines from dunking donuts into creamy coffee and talking too much. How I was wrong. That's just how parents were. My mom had warned me not to go to Club Estrella, while Dad, his hand on the remote control, offered up only his hangdog eyes.

Soon we were entering Roeding Park from Olive Street. An unseen peacock howled.

"Spooky," I remarked.

Crystal had to laugh. "Like us, huh?" She laughed with a hand on her belly. "We're ghosts!"

The wind rattled the eucalyptus and bent the thinnest branches. Leaves fluttered in the dark as they fell. Somewhere a swing squeaked. The door of a utility shed banged like a hammer. Though it was dark and the homeless were sleeping on cardboard the length of coffins, we weren't scared. The ducks weren't either. Some were quacking and waddling around, though they should have been asleep at the edges of their muddy pond. In a few hours, the ducks would be poking their bills into their feathery shoulders and riding the mossy water in search of food.

We flowed over the wet lawn and, for the fun of it, rode a merry-go-round that was pushed by the wind. Crystal's hair flowed and her face was a blossom of happiness. I loved her. I wanted to say as much, but what good would it do? A lot, for me at least. But the time was not right; after all, we were in search of the place where she had died, for her body.

We flew from that merry-go-round across the park. We stopped and hovered near a homeless man propped against a tree, shivering. A dirty blanket covered him up to his throat.

"What's wrong with him?" Crystal asked, worried.

The man was sick with fever and more than sick: He was a homeless guy who was dying.

"He's dying," I answered.

I stepped back, scared. His ghost was starting to peel away from his body. It started to rise, but I quickly got down on my knees and applied my stumps to cool the man's fever. *Don't die,* I begged. *Please don't die.* I touched his face with my stumps, pulled them away, and applied them again.

I had never seen anyone die before, and I didn't want to start right then. I applied my cool ghostliness to his forehead. The man was funky smelling, his teeth nearly orange as Cheetos. I noticed that a part of his earlobe was gone. The man, it seemed, had had a rough life.

I glanced over my shoulder. Crystal was biting the ends of her hair, a bad habit. Leaves were falling through her body. That seemed like a habit, too—things passing through us because we were ghosts with the weight of smoke.

"Is he going to be okay?" Crystal asked.

Okay? I wondered. *Probably not. What man parks his body against a tree at night?*

Slowly the ghost that he was giving up receded back into his body. He moaned with relief and tossed his head side to side. His shivering began to lessen.

I stood up and flowed to Crystal, and together we watched the man sleep, his fever having broken. His breathing was even, and when he cranked out a nasty snore, we had to laugh. He was sick, we knew, but in the morning he would have to figure out whether to drag himself to a clinic or just lie against the tree and wait for his ghost—his afterlife—to resurface and rise from his body. It was up to him.

"Let's go," I suggested. "I don't know what else to do."

It was still dark among the trees, whose tops were thrashing about, but I could tell that the sky was becoming pale in the east. Crystal led me through the park, confused about where she had parked her car. Then we found it by the tennis courts. Beads of dew frosted the front window. We approached slowly. Crystal lowered her head. If she could have produced tears, she would have dampened the lawn with her sadness.

The police hadn't yet found her car or her body.

"I can't look," Crystal cried. She spun away and walked inside a eucalyptus tree, its thickness absorbing her.

I was full of distress, too. I considered walking inside the same tree to see if we fit, one girl and one boy. Instead, I sat on top of a bench and remembered when I was little and how Eddie and I used to play "pretend dead." Shot by imaginary gangsters, we would topple on the grass and see who looked more dead than the other—I had my little trick of keeping my eyes open and staring at the sky motionless. And Eddie? I couldn't do what he did. He would let flies crawl on his face. Once, a mosquito even landed on his throat and starting pumping away. Did Eddie slap that vampire of insects into a bloody mess? *Chale!* No way.

Finally, Crystal emerged from the tree. She pulled her hair behind her ear. We held and rocked each other as if we were slow dancing. In fact, we might have been slow dancing to some rhythm inside our head. In that position, I asked her: "Why did you kill yourself? You're so beautiful."

"You think so?" she asked, her head turned slightly away. She doubted her own natural beauty.

I kissed her neck and breathed in her ear. "Are you kidding?"

She lowered her face into my shoulder, a new sensation for me, one that made my back and shoulders quiver. God, a young woman crying into my shoulder. Most of the ones I met wouldn't let me hold their hand, let alone share with me their grief. But this was so different. I hugged her tenderly, and glanced over her shoulder at the car, where the Crystal that most of the world knew was slumped. I realized I didn't want to see her that way. At the moment, I didn't care how she died. The cops, though, would want to know everything. And they would. It was dark now, but once the eyelid of night rose on a new day, some early-morning jogger would come across her body. The one in the car, not the one leaning into my shoulders.

SELMA, RAISIN CAPITAL OF THE WORLD. That's what the bullet-pierced sign read as Crystal and I approached the outskirts of a city that still smelled of harvested grapes. The vines, however, were bare, the leaves having fallen and scuttled to wherever leaves go. At one farm, I spotted a rabbit running between rows. The rabbit was followed by another rabbit, then still another. Life was multiplying right before my eyes, it seemed.

It was getting light. The eastern horizon was

pinkish, though the big-eyed sun had yet to show itself and wrap the valley in its autumn warmth. Because we were in the country, roosters were stirring up the air with their racket. A few dogs, too, were yapping about the start of a new day. A tractor was starting up with loud, smoky coughs. So this was country life. It was neither beautiful nor quiet as on TV. What did TV know about *los campos,* the fields? I had to admit that I wasn't an expert, either. I had worked just six weeks in the grape fields. There wouldn't be any work today, or very little. It was Sunday. Most fieldworkers were in bed, some snoring off hangovers and others resting their bones.

At that early hour, I imagined priests, awake but tired as well, sitting at large oak tables writing on lined paper: "Jesus has risen." Heck, they might have been talking about me, because didn't I share His name—Jesús, though I was better known as Chuy? And hadn't I also risen, though instead of in a tomb my resurrection took place on a dirty floor? But unlike the son of God who washed away all our sins, I wasn't going to be around long. That was clear when I saw that my legs were gone up to my knees. Most of my forearms were gone, too.

"Chuy!" Crystal cried.

At first, I assumed her outburst was meant for me. But I was wrong. Crystal was examining her feet—the tips of her toes were gone. Soon the whole of her two feet would disappear and then she would be like me.

Then Crystal saw me. "Oh, Chuy," she cried. She had noticed that more of me was lopped off.

I wish I could have been braver and made a silly remark like, "Don't worry, baby. It ain't nothing." But it *was* something. I was worried that I might disappear altogether before I could force my mom to take back that handgun from Eddie. Why get him involved in my bad luck? After all, I was the loudmouth who made the mistake of complimenting some dude for having nice shoes. What kind of words could I use to tell my mom to please, for God's sake, go get that gun from Eddie? What parts of my ghostly body would there be left after I saw Crystal home?

But I did groan, "Ah, man, look at me now!" My ghostly eyes must have given away my fear. Crystal could see this. She hugged me and I did my best to return her gesture.

"I love you, baby," I said. "Come on, show me where you live. I want to see your ribbons."

Crystal smiled, eye cocked at what she perceived as my naughtiness. "You mean you want to see my bedroom. That's where they are."

Her bedroom! *Yeah,* I thought. *I want to see her bedroom.*

Crystal released me with a single kiss on my throat, and began to run in long, beautiful strides, which I recognized as the graceful movements of a true distance runner. I never had those kinds of strides when I ran for my school, and I didn't have them now.

The sun was bloodred in the east, and the first newspapers were being delivered. But the news of her death would not be there. If the police hadn't located her car at Roeding Park, they wouldn't know about her death either. But I was certain that her parents were up, dressed, and pacing the house or the police station. After all, their daughter never came home.

She was coming now, but how would they recognize her, this ghostly Crystal with the bad habit of biting the ends of her hair and letting leaves fall through her?

CHAPTER
Seven

I REMEMBER Dad saying that life is a journey that ends in the same place where you begin. He was philosophizing after the Raiders lost a playoff game—the attempted field goal that would have put the team up by one point hit the uprights and bounced left, also bouncing the air out of every Raider fan from Oakland to Los Angeles. That late afternoon, his eyes were misty with sadness, his jowls heavy with disappointment. His breath thick and beery. I don't believe Dad knew what he was talking about. He was just moving his lips.

I was moving my lips, too, muttering, "No way," because the unlikely occurred. Crystal lived on the farm where I had worked picking grapes when I was twelve. Maybe that's what Dad meant—or sort of meant—when he said that life brings you back to the same place. I stood neck deep in vines that were stripped of leaves, revealing bunches of grapes missed by the pickers. I gawked at an older but well-kept white house with a wraparound porch. A dusty but newish truck sat in the driveway. A chained dog slept in a puddle of morning sunlight.

"What a trip," I remarked, and approached the house.

I remember the house and a girl—Crystal?—reclining in a chair and reading a magazine as I went to hose my face after I got stung by a wasp. I remember she glanced up, pushed up a small but sincere smile at poor me, and immediately cast her eyes down again at whatever she was reading. Even then, with my swollen face, I was in love with her, or in love with someone who could kick it on a porch, an icy soda at her side.

That was five years ago. Now I was hovering off the driveway in front of a house that seemed empty. Crystal had flown ahead of me because she wanted to visit her parents alone. She would sit with them in the living room sharing their sadness. In her own way, she might apologize for killing herself.

I considered climbing the front porch but instead ventured around to the barn to confirm my belief that this was the same family farm. I looked up at the rafters and flew to the eaves where I made out a row of honeycombs, little gray houses where wasps snuggled to bed. A few wasps flew through me like needles, as if they were sewing me up. A pair of bats, like pieces of dark fruit, hung under there, too. But the bats were asleep, their paper-thin wings like a blanket around their eyes.

"This has to got to be the place," I uttered to myself. I felt a weird joy.

Flying, I scanned the vineyards. At the end of one row, a crazy dust twister was lifting up sand. When I was a kid, I used to see these heat-created twisters in the country. Once, when my dad had pulled off the road because of a flat, a twister popped up out of nowhere. When it approached our car, I did what any other kid would do: I jumped in its center, thinking about *The Wizard of Oz* and ending up in a magical place. The only place I ended up was in the backseat of the car, Dad hollering at me because I had sand in my hair, my eyes, and even my *chones*.

This twister, however, quickly died.

I flew to the end of the farm's property and back to the house, where I encountered Crystal sitting on the front porch. She was chewing a fingernail. I figured that her mom and dad weren't home, but instead were at the police station, maybe the hospital. I sat next to her, and didn't say a word when I noticed that both her feet were gone—she was disappearing more quickly than me. We sat in silence, with wind whistling through the stripped vines.

"I never liked my feet," Crystal finally said. "They were ugly."

I couldn't believe any part of Crystal was ugly. I was liking her more and more and believing we were meant for each other.

"No way," I argued. "You had pretty feet."

Crystal rose and manufactured a smile that was mechanical, forced. Still, I liked it a lot and followed her as she went through the front door. The living room was dark with shadows in spite of the lamp that was on and the feathery sunlight cast on the wall. The furniture was nice and everything was in its place, clean. A large clock in the shape of a sunflower hummed atop the TV. On the wall hung a reproduction of a painting I remembered from history and from Kmart. I winced as I tried to remember its name.

"It's *The Blue Boy*," Crystal filled in for me. "Gainsborough."

"Man, I knew what picture it was," I lied. "And the dude who did it!"

The next smile Crystal gave me was sweet and sincere. So was her description of me. "You liar," she uttered softly, and rubbed her nose against mine.

Hijole! I was making headway with her!

I followed Crystal down the hall, aware of where we were going—her bedroom. I imagined it was pink and frilly. But first we stopped and gazed at the telephone in the hallway. It was blinking three messages. Then a telephone in another part of the house began to ring. Quickly Crystal hurried into her bedroom and stood over her own phone. On the third ring, the message machine kicked in, "Hey, I'm not here. But I'd like to hear from you." Then a voice said in a whisper, "Crystal, it's me, Jason."

Crystal reached to pick up the phone not once but twice, but had no power to lift it to her ear. It was her boyfriend, I was sure, and to give her privacy I returned to the living room, where I watched the action inside a fishbowl. Two goldfish were throwing up bubbles that broke on the surface.

Still, I heard the message. It was from her boyfriend who sounded nervous because Crystal's dad and mom had shown up at his house asking about her. He said that they were just leaving. Crystal made a remark about being sorry.

Crystal emerged from her bedroom and said, "Let's go."

"No, let's wait for your mom and dad to come back," I suggested.

"No," she snapped, "let's go!"

The telephone in the hallway began to ring and beg for attention. On the third ring, the answering machine picked up: "Sorry, we're not here to take your call, but if you leave a clear and well-spoken message we'll be sure to get back to you." The voice belonged to her mom. The somber voice that came on belonged to the police. "Mr. and Mrs. Kerr, we would appreciate a call from you if you're home. Also..." There was a squawk of a radio. "A sheriff in your area is going to come by..."

It was clear to me, and it was clear to Crystal. They had found her body. The police were saying as much.

"I'm sorry," I mumbled to Crystal.

"But you already know that I'm dead."

This was true. I was sorry for her parents. I imagined the crumbling when the news got to them. I swallowed. I had no moisture in my swallow or water and salt to form a single tear. *Their daughter,* I thought. *Dead over a boy.* Why did she do that? I would have loved her. Hell, I would have picked those grapes for the rest of my life for her love. I opened my mouth and told her so.

"Right," she said, blowing me off with a single word. She was worried for her parents. Or was it her boyfriend?

"I love you a lot," I argued, then pouted. *God, if I could only grow a second pair of arms to hug her.* I hesitated before I told her, "You won't believe this, but I worked on your dad's farm."

"You're full of lies." She propped her hands on her hips.

"No, I did, really."

Her arms moved from her hips to across her chest, a sign that she didn't believe me.

"Dad brought me here when I was twelve. He said he wanted me to know what it was to work with my hands." I looked down at where my hands might have been attached.

Crystal huffed.

"And I remember you." I recalled the day the wasp had stung me and how I saw her on the porch. She had everything—magazines, sodas, even her daddy's cell phone. "You were so spoiled."

"Me? Spoiled?" She pointed a thumb at her heart. A little smirk at the corner of her mouth gave her away. "Maybe."

"Yeah, you were. Kicking back while us Mexicans were working in the field." I was going to take my argument as far as it could go.

"*Us* Mexicans? I'm Mexican, too."

"Get out of here." It never occurred to me that she could be *raza*. Her hair was light brown and her skin was freckled along the tops of her arms. But suddenly her face became Mexican, and lovelier.

"Half Mexican, at least. My mom is Mexican . . . I can even make tortillas."

I laughed. Make tortillas? I would have continued laughing except the telephone started ringing again. We both stared at it, and before the message machine kicked in, we were out the front door and down the porch, both of us throwing ourselves skyward and flying. We didn't need the answering machine to tell us what we knew already, that Crystal was dead. At my side, she seemed more than alive enough to me.

I TRAILED Crystal over one family farm after another, avoiding the twisters that stirred the brittle autumn leaves like cornflakes. I churned my legs and flapped the stumps of my arms to keep up. Crystal was not only a good runner, but she could move sweetly in the air. I was so in love with her, but did she care? The girl was fast, eager, and thoughtless—she had to be aware that I knew where we were headed. Her boyfriend Jason's crib.

"Your parents aren't going to be there," I shouted. My strategy was to get her mind off her boyfriend and change our course back to her farm.

Crystal ignored me.

Her boyfriend lived in town in a house that looked like mine, down to the rosebushes and the shaggy mint growing by the front faucet, where the garden hose was rolled up all nice. But I didn't have time to assess the house like a real estate agent because her boyfriend—the dude was good-looking, and strong—came out of the house shrugging into his letterman's jacket. His sport, I could see, was football. I then noticed the crosshatched emblems of baseball bats on his chest. There were medals, too, and a couple of pins I couldn't read. He was a hero in all seasons!

I fell from the sky, hurt that the guy was a stud. And me? In life I was just an ordinary kid named Chuy with faded third-place ribbons back in his bedroom. The only part of my body I could brag about was my stomach—it was flat and a valley when I lay down. But what of it? I couldn't go around pulling up my shirt and crowing, "Hey, check out my abs, homeboys."

I nearly begged Crystal to go back to her house—her parents would be returning home to the messages on the answering machine—but I recognized in her face that she had something to share with him. I guess it wasn't my business. I could have flown away, or rolled like a tumbleweed back to Fresno. But, no, I joined Crystal, who sat shotgun in her boyfriend's tricked-out Honda. Shamelessly, I sat in the back as her boyfriend, eyes raised up to the rearview mirror, backed out of the driveway recklessly, nearly hitting the trash can on the curb. He wrestled with the steering wheel as he roared down the street, scattering leaves and a cat orange as a pumpkin—and nearly bloody as a pomegranate if he hadn't scampered quickly.

"Did his mommy buy his car?" I taunted. "His daddy?" I was full of envy. He had a car, a letterman's jacket dangling with medals and stuff, and, of course, the memory of Crystal in his arms.

Crystal whipped her head around and gave me a mean look, the kind my mom gave me when she wanted me to shut up.

But I didn't shut up. "What's he better at, football or baseball?"

"He's not the boyfriend you're thinking about."

Not the boyfriend you're thinking about, I mused. What did that mean?

"You don't understand."

I had heard that line before and used it, too, mainly on my parents. Jealous that she was riding up front with Jason, I pouted and watched the houses pass in a blur. This dude was speeding at an hour in the morning when people were off for church or bringing out their mowers for a trim of the quickly dying autumn lawns.

After a straight line across Selma, hardly braking at the two stop signs, both riddled with bullet holes, Crystal's boyfriend pulled up in front of a rich person's house. How could I tell? There were two Lexuses in the driveway and what looked like a

Porsche under a cover. On the porch stood two cut pumpkins, one smiling and the other making a long, ugly face.

"Who lives here?" I asked Crystal, who had her face buried in her hands.

"No," she cried. "Leave him alone, Eric."

"No, what? What's wrong?"

"It's Jason's house," she stammered.

"Jason? I thought this dude was Jason."

Confused, I got out of the car when the stud got out of the car. He muttered juvenile-level cuss words, and marched toward the front door. But he didn't have to knock, because another kid his age— my age—in another lettermen's jacket came out, his fists closing and his jaw set. Neither said a word as they started hitting each other violently. The medals on their chest jangled like keys.

Dawg, I thought, jumping up so that I hung in the air.

They battered each other for a few furious minutes and then took off their jackets to really get to work. With each strike, blood flowed, hair bounced, bone crushed, and air left their guts. They muttered threats and groans and savage remarks about each other's mothers. I was glad right there and then that I didn't have to defend my mother's honor. These two were vicious.

"Who's the other dude?" I yelled at Crystal, who

was still sitting in the front seat of the car. Her head was bobbing as she sobbed. She refused to explain.

A neighbor, in his old-man slippers, came out, yelling for both of them to stop. They listened to the neighbor for a second, snorting like bulls. Their breath was hot from wherever anger and hate dwells inside the body.

"Jason, what is this about?" asked the neighbor. He had it all wrong. Jason was the dude I rode in the car with—no?

The two jocks caught their breath. Then they started again, this time with wild kicks, none of which connected solidly. They were out of gas. Their blows slowed and then picked up, then slowed again as the blood in their veins couldn't carry enough oxygen to help them really hurt each other.

They stopped fighting and stared at each other.

"She didn't come home last night," Jason said after he gathered enough air in his lungs to form that one sentence. He caught more air and asked. "Is she with you?"

"Nah, she ain't with me. Her parents came over and were asking about her, but I told them that she was probably with you."

I still couldn't figure out what was going on.

"Stop it, Eric!" Crystal screamed. She had gotten out of the car, and not by conventional means. She flew up through the roof.

The neighbor was right. The dude who came out of the house was named Jason, and I figured the other dude was Eric, the dude who drove us here.

"Eric, leave Jason alone!" Crystal shouted, but who could hear a ghost?

I would have scratched my head, but I had no fingers. So I screamed at Crystal, "Who are these dudes?"

"My boyfriends," she sobbed.

Dawg, I thought. *The girl's got two boyfriends—no, three, counting me if I had my way.* And I could! I realized I was in a better situation than either of them. I was a ghost while they were torn flesh, hurt bone, and spilled blood at the moment. But they could easily become ghosts, the way they were going.

Eric threw a lovely roundhouse punch that sent Jason down for the count. He staggered backward and fell into a sitting position on the front lawn. He was out cold, sitting up, eyes closed, and nobody home.

"I want you to leave her alone," Eric threatened. "She's my girl!" By mistake he picked up the letterman's jacket that belonged to Jason and hurried to his car.

God help them, I prayed, when they got the word of Crystal's suicide. Each one would think that it was his own fault, or maybe the other person's fault.

Would they go to the funeral, and if they did, would they be wearing each other's jacket and the same look of gloom?

I ALWAYS DREAMED about sleeping in a pile of hay in the arms of someone I loved. Actually, not sleeping but lolling groggily on a natural mattress. Now I was. I was lying side by side with Crystal in a horse pasture, but had no arms to embrace her. If I had, I'm not sure she would have let me. She just lay at my side staring at the sky that held two clouds. It was already late afternoon, and soon the evening would descend like a cloak. But for the time being, I was next to her and I didn't give a shit whether she had two boyfriends or ten. In fact, I was mad at them because one of them—maybe both of them—had led her to kill herself. It had to be about those jocks who were now at their separate homes staring at their letterman's jackets and thinking, *Jesus, the other dude's got mine.* That would mean they would have to meet again and swap a few blows. I figured, let them hurt each other. Let their perfect jock smiles be ruined. As for me, I had Crystal, or sort of. When I reached over, she turned her face away from me. She was thinking of home and, maybe, why she committed suicide over two jocks.

"Crystal," I whispered.

"What?" she asked after a moment of silence. She turned her face back to me. We were so close we were seeing cross-eyed.

"Why did you have two boyfriends?"

"I was popular." She said this with a straight face and then laughed with one hand on her belly and the other shading her eyes.

"Come on, homegirl."

She wiped the corner of her eye, as if a tear of laughter had crawled out. "It's true."

I sat up, grinning. "You think you're something, huh?" She *was* something.

Crystal sat up. "Yeah, I'm something, or I was until I killed myself."

"Over Jason and Eric. They're nowhere." Of course, in my heart, I realized that they were studs and maybe even really decent at heart. And they could both fight.

"No, I killed myself because . . ." Crystal turned away from me.

"What?" I asked, and rolled over her ghostly body to face her. I liked her nose, delicate as porcelain, whereas mine was like a spud, a *papa*.

"Because I didn't think I was going to do it." She swallowed and added, "You know, make it big in life, like Martha Stewart or Oprah. I could make it big here in Selma, but not in New York."

The whole world knew Oprah, but who was this Martha Stewart? She had the name of a dead president's wife. "You were going to go to New York?"

Crystal frowned at me. "You don't get it, buster." She rambled on that it could be Chicago or San Francisco or Los Angeles. The city didn't matter. What mattered was making it. She would be small in a new place, just a little ant carrying her briefcase to work. Wherever she was going, she doubted that she could demand the same attention as in Selma, where she was vice president of her school, a cheerleader, a nearly straight-A student, and even a member of 4-H. She told me she had applied to Harvard and Stanford and got rejected. She was going to USC.

"Hey, I was nowhere all my life. It wasn't that bad." I bragged that if I had lived, I would have attended Fresno City College.

Crystal fumed. "Don't you understand? I got rejected!"

Dawg, I thought. She was scared of failing. So that was it.

We lay staring at the sky, both of us quiet. The two clouds were gone, the sky darker now that the sun was eclipsed by a walnut tree.

"Crystal," I meowed romantically. I turned my face to her. "You know I like you."

Crystal blinked her eyes at the sky.

But my mood shifted quickly. "But I got to go see someone at my house." I was up. "Plus, you were going to see about your parents."

At the word *parents,* Crystal rolled into a ball on that haystack.

"Crystal," I called softly.

"What," she answered, not so softly.

"I went to see my grandfather. He died six years ago of cancer." I told her that I was probably going to be buried there, in the same cemetery. I told her it was kind of nice, with trees and lawns that were cut weekly.

Crystal sat up, her legs folded in a yoga position. Her face was lined with worry. "I guess you and I are going to disappear, huh? Like, really disappear." She swallowed that truth. "Like really die, huh?"

I listened to a distant airplane. A bird on the barbed wire fence. A horse whinny. These were the sounds that are singled out in the country, especially on a pile of hay that either a horse would eat or the wind carry away, flake by flake. I wish we could have lain there forever.

"I have a confession," Crystal began. Her face had brightened.

"What, another boyfriend?"

She smiled. "Sort of," she teased.

I held my breath. Was she messing around with *all* of Selma?

"I remember you."

I offered her a confused look. I didn't get what she was saying, though it had to be good because her face was open and beautiful.

"I remember when you were picking grapes and got stung." She pulled her hair behind her eyes. "I thought you were cute."

I smiled. "You don't really remember, do you?" I asked. "You're just playing with me!"

"Yeah, I do!" Her smile was like a flower.

"And I was cute?" I was really begging for a compliment.

Crystal rose and hugged and kissed me. "Yes, you were cute. Even with your fat swollen face."

We gazed into each other's eyes until we were both out of focus. I then pulled away from her as I repeated that I had to go back home and take care of business. I sailed into a sky that was bloodred where the sun was going down. I turned and yelled, "I'll be back." I would have waved but my arms were gone. I told her that I loved her, but my words were snapped up by the heartless wind.

CHAPTER
Eight

USK BROUGHT the cries of peacocks sailing across the scraggly lawns of Roeding Park. I kicked down the street where, the night before, Crystal's car had sat with Crystal inside, dead. The police and an ambulance had come and gone along with a tow truck that hauled her ride away. I stared at a blotch of oil.

"Ah, Crystal," I cried, then pivoted and walked toward a group of young trees where darkness was knitting the oncoming night.

I pictured her mom crying into her hands, and her dad leaning his shoulder against a wall, his closed fists wiping a couple of tears that would replenish themselves when he was asked to view her body. I pictured her two boyfriends, Jason and Eric, going through the school yearbook in search of pictures of her.

"Ah, Crystal," I repeated, head down. I looked up when a wind reshuffled the leaves on the lawn. Before me lay the homeless guy whom I had saved by cooling his hot forehead. He had died after all and was now a ghost, too. I wasn't surprised at all.

"I tried," I told him, stepping toward him. What could I fear from him or anyone else?

"You were the one?" he asked.

I nodded my head.

"I remember someone trying to help me."

The ghost was younger than the bag of bones that had leaned against the tree. I could see that when older people died and became a ghost they took on a younger appearance, not a final road-weary flesh. I was still learning about death.

"You had a fever," I explained. The memory of his ghost lifting from his body was etched in my mind. "I tried to help you, sir."

"Yeah, I was sick and had this fever for two days," the man explained. "But I was just tired of it all." He grumbled about people going camping and how he had been doing it for ten years. But his camping, he argued, was homelessness. He wanted to sleep in a bed. He asked my name.

"Chuy," I answered.

He munched on the inside of his lower lip as he considered my name. He was calm for being a ghost. When I was on the roof of Club Estrella and examining my body right after I died, I was tripped out by my new status as ghost. In fact, at that time, there was no fear in me, nor a sense of loss, not like now. I was suffering over the loss of Crystal and the wide expanse of the years I didn't get to live. I asked his name.

"Robert Montgomery," he answered. "Like the actor."

"What actor?"

"What do you mean, 'What actor?' *The* actor!" This Robert Montgomery, tall and lean, scratched his chin. He was puzzled that I didn't recognize the name. "I guess he might have been before your time."

We watched a cop car pass, its backseat vacant but ready to be filled because the cop, a young one, was looking for trouble. Anything to bring his nightstick like a saber from his holster. When the cruiser disappeared from sight, I braved the question. "Ain't it weird that you died and came back? That you're a ghost?"

"Nah, not really. I always felt like a ghost anyway, because people would look through me all the time."

I understood what he was saying. Because he was a homeless guy, people walked by as if he were invisible. I was not righteous, because I had walked by the homeless, too, indifferent to the chant of "spare change." My dad taught me to avoid them. He argued that they were too lazy to work.

He pointed toward the road. "You know, I saw this girl kill herself."

I jerked.

"She was really young." He seemed remorseful that he hadn't been able to help Crystal.

We drifted toward the road.

"I went up to the car," he continued, "and she was crying. She had taken something." He became silent and closed his eyes to mutter a prayer. With his eyes closed, he added, "I think she regretted what she had done, but there was nothing she could do, or I could do. The stuff was in her system."

I envisioned Crystal in the car and the pills she had gulped like breath mints. Maybe she was listening to music as she went under. Maybe she was holding a rosary or a photo of her family. I considered telling this newly dead man, this ghost, that I loved her. But I remained quiet and shut my eyes for a short prayer.

"Yeah, the cops came and they took her away and then they saw me right there." He pointed to the tree where he had rested in fever. "Saved the cops the trouble of coming back and picking me up. The city ought to give me an award!" He laughed and did a little dance. The guy, it seemed, was what my dad would call a character.

When a peacock cried a haunting scream, Robert screamed and scampered inside the tree he was standing next to.

"Robert!" I called. "That bird ain't gonna hurt you. Come on out!"

He behaved himself and came out, looking nervously about for the peacock. "Man, it's weird that we can go through things."

"You're a ghost," I told him. "You're like smoke, but better than smoke. You can go into anything you want."

"Can I fly?" He stretched out his arms and flapped them as if I didn't understand his question.

"Yeah, but you don't go very fast."

He laughed, and wagged a threatening finger at the peacock and made a chopping motion with his hand. He could have whacked and whacked, but his efforts would have been meaningless. His powerless hand had the weight of air. "So what goes?"

I didn't understand.

"We're dead, and now what?" he asked. He was examining the stumps of my arms and my legs that were almost all gone. The guy was not discreet. "You look like someone chopped part of you off. Is that how you died?"

I shook my head. "Someone stabbed me."

Robert pondered my murder for a moment, a hand smoothing his hair. "Someone stabbed me, too." He explained that it was over what mattered most to him—a bottle of wine.

"And you lived?" I asked.

"Oh, yeah. He stabbed me in the shoulder—the dummy missed my throat—and I hit him with a brick that dropped him pretty good. I finished my drink all by myself."

So here was my new companion. I repeated my name again when he asked it, and informed him that I had been a ghost for two days, almost three. I grew fearful. I remembered that I didn't have much time before I would disappear altogether, just vanish. I still wanted to tell my mom and dad that I loved them, to see Angel and Eddie, the four Js, maybe Rachel. I started to walk away.

"Where you going?" Robert asked.

"Home."

"Home," he repeated softly. He smacked his lips as if he could taste home.

His longing was familiar. Crystal suffered from that longing, and I had suffered it, too. Home is what ghosts seek out after they die—it was just natural.

"But I don't know what home is," he confessed. He briefed me on the years he'd spent at three or four foster homes, and he didn't care for any of them, though at one home the foster mother cooked a nice chicken dinner every Friday. He smacked his lips as if he were tasting it again.

When I asked if he had been born in Fresno, he answered, nearly insulted, "Yeah, of course." As if Fresno was the only place to be born.

We left the park and immediately got onto a bus that was so bright we had to shade our eyes. Though we were the only passengers, we took a seat in the back where candy wrappers and potato chip bags gathered. It was in the light of that moving bus that Robert got another eyeful of me.

"You really do got no legs," he said sorrowfully. "Or arms." He shook his head and bit his lower lip. He went into himself, his face dark in spite of the light.

"I'm disappearing," I said without explanation.

Robert bowed his head. He felt terrible for me. "God, you were only a young man. Who killed you?"

"Some dude," I answered. I imagined a pair of yellow shoes. I recalled how he wiped his blade on my shirt and hissed in my ear, "What did you say to me, *cabrón?*"

"I'm really sorry," Robert cooed. He put an arm around my shoulder.

"Bad luck," I said, snuggling up to him because he needed friendship more than me. It had probably been years since anyone sat close to him.

"I got stabbed," he said, "and I lived."

"You told me already."

His eyes rolled in their sockets. "Oh, yeah, I did, didn't I?" Even as a ghost his memory was ruined from drinking cheap stuff. "Hey, did I tell you that I once slept on a bus like this for twelve hours straight?"

I shook my head.

"Yeah, I paid once and got to ride the bus all day. It was raining. I guess the bus driver felt sorry for me."

As the bus rolled down the street, occasionally hitting a pothole, I had to wonder about what I called my bad luck. How was it that some dudes got stabbed and shot and lived? How did the Almighty decide? If I had stayed home on Friday night, I would be with Angel right now at the end of a glorious Sunday. We would be grass-stained from neighborhood football, and our worst wounds would be from getting our butts whipped, our pride dented. Our Sunday football game would have been dinner conversation since our families—he at his place, me at mine—liked to eat as a family on Sunday evenings.

The bus braked and sighed. I watched a dude swagger onto the bus, his pants all *huango,* his eyes narrow, sunflower seed shells spraying from his mouth. It was Yellow Shoes!

"Get back here!" the bus driver bellowed. His eyes were raised to the rearview mirror. If he was married and had a son, I guaranteed that son would perk up when his dad spoke.

"What you want?" Yellow Shoes bawled without respect.

"For you to drop some coins into this thing." The driver, a black man with a belt of fat around his middle, wasn't someone to play with. He pounded a giant fist on the meter that gobbled coins and dollar bills. The bus didn't get about on courtesy. No, it ran on money, hard-earned or stolen. I was sure the coins that Yellow Shoes let fall from his tattooed fingers were stolen.

At first, I didn't say anything to Robert, who was staring out the window at two men carrying a couch down the sidewalk—the couch was either stolen or bought at a yard sale. Instead, I slid out of my seat and approached Yellow Shoes, who had fit headphones over his oily ears.

"You're a punk," I growled. I remembered that he and I shared the same name. I suddenly hated my name—Chuy—and hated the music that was coming out of his headphones. The beat was loud and stupid.

Alert, Robert got up and approached us. He had lived on the street for years and was a better judge of character than most people. He gave Yellow Shoes a mean look. "Is he the one?"

I nodded my head.

"Does he still have the knife on him?"

"Nah, he tossed it."

The bus rolled on, its springs squeaky over the rough road.

"So what powers do we got?" Robert asked.

"What do you mean?"

"Can we hurt him? Jack him up?" He hooked a thumb at Yellow Shoes.

Hurt him? I hadn't thought of revenge and, actually, was trying to keep Eddie, my *primo*, from seeking revenge. Now this man whom I had saved wanted to do away with Yellow Shoes.

"Nah, we can't do anything," I answered. I didn't want to let on that we ghosts could cause mayhem with the living.

"What an ugly face!" Robert snarled.

"Yeah, *muy* ugly."

We returned to our seat. The bus stopped and two kids with skateboards hopped on, laughing. They were dirty but good kids, like Angel and me at one time. Their elbows and knees were bloody from falling, their palms black with oily grime from gripping the bottoms of their boards.

"What you lookin' at, white boy?" Yellow Shoes taunted. He pulled the headphones from his ears. His rat face twitched.

The boys' only response was to backtrack and sit closer to the driver.

"I said, what you lookin' at?" Yellow Shoes hollered.

The kids, skateboards pressed between their knees, looked straight ahead. They took a sudden interest in the car the bus trailed.

"I hate that kid," Robert growled. He turned to me. "He killed you and you don't want to do anything about it?" Robert wagged his head in disgust that could have been directed either at me or at Yellow Shoes. "In my time—"

I cut him off. "I don't want to talk about it." I fumed as I thought of Fausto, bike thief and thug of all thugs. I had a great, painful urge to erase him and Yellow Shoes from the face of our dirty little planet. I boiled with a sudden hatred.

The bus rolled for a mile, but no one else boarded. In Fresno, everyone owned a car. If you didn't, you were elderly, young, disabled, or truly poor.

Robert nudged me. "You sure you never heard of Robert Montgomery? He was a famous actor. Think he won an Oscar, the whole enchilada."

"Nah, never heard of him."

"That's good then," Robert said. "Because now you can just remember me, okay?"

I was confused.

Robert rose from our seat, sidled up to Yellow Shoes, and slowly stepped into my killer's skin, as if he were slipping into one of those black diving suits. Robert's head stuck out of Yellow Shoes's body, two heads on a single set of shoulders.

"I'm going to stir up this little fool," Robert said. He offered up a sorrowful good-bye with a wink of an eye. "Remember me. See you on the other side."

The other side, I wondered. *What is on the other side?*

Robert disappeared into Yellow Shoes's body, not unlike how he stepped inside the tree. Yellow Shoes quivered, juiced up by the sudden appearance of another soul inside him. He looked sick, scared. A sunflower seed shell fell from his lips. He let the bag of sunflower seeds spill to the floor. "Bus driver, I don't feel good!" Yellow Shoes threw his head into the window. The thud left a greasy smear on the glass. He thrashed about. His legs fanned in and out.

This commotion brought the bus driver's eyes to the rearview mirror.

Yellow Shoes stood up, then sat back down. His teeth chattered like castanets. His knees went up and down like pistons. I thought of the movie *The Exorcist.* Was his head going to twist and spray vomit? At the thought, I got up and jumped from the bus as it was moving. I didn't want to see any more. I rolled twice and righted myself in front of a paint store with graffiti on the front. I had never been a hero, though I can say that I saved a man who shared a name with an actor I had never heard of. Then again, I never heard of ghosts who were willing to crawl into another body. Especially a killer's body.

"Dawg," I muttered.

The bus braked and the two kids jumped off the bus, their skateboards hitting the pavement. They were sailing from trouble on a Sunday evening when the sky was boiling with rain clouds.

EDDIE'S APARTMENT. A black suit was laid out like a shadow on his couch. It was from the Salvation Army, I noticed by the tag attached to the sleeve, but the white shirt was new and still in its package. A pair of shoes that needed polishing lay at the cuffs of the pants. All that was needed was Eddie's body to fill those clothes with the warmth of his flesh. I wondered what kind of suit my mom got me. A black one like Eddie's? Or was she going to use the brown one I bought last year for the fall dance?

I sat on the couch and swallowed my fear. It tasted like wet earth. When was I going to be buried? Monday? Tuesday? I yearned to make my rounds once more in Fresno and beg—but how?—that my mother leave Eddie alone. Why should he seek revenge?

The telephone began to ring. I got up and found it in the kitchen sitting next to a toaster. His machine kicked in: "This is Eddie. You know what to do, man." *Beep.* Then my mother's voice in a whisper: "Eddie, you can find him, *mi'jo.* Please find him. I have more bullets if you need more. I'll see you at the rosary in a little bit." There was the sound of a television in the background. Then the final prodding: "*Mi'jo,* he loved you a lot. He would do it for you."

My mom's voice was spooky and her message even scarier. I imagined her completing this call and shuffling back to her couch, where she would pick up her knitting needles. *Maybe she was knitting a ski mask for Eddie,* I mused. No telling who's who in that getup.

I turned and jumped when I spied the towel my mom used to carry the gun. The gun wasn't there, though.

"Mom!" I scolded. "Why get Eddie involved?"

I imagined the gun cradled in the pouch of Eddie's Fresno State Bulldog sweatshirt. I imagined the bullets oily and merciless in their drive to hurt someone.

Next to the towel lay a newspaper article reporting my murder. The suspect, the article said, was Hispanic, early twenties, and lean, with a shaved head. It could have been anyone, even me, and this frightened me. At that moment, Eddie could be tracking down my killer on such vague details. I figured that he could shoot in the sky and the bullet that came down would most likely hit an unlucky soul who fit the description.

The article also announced my rosary at Everlasting Light Mortuary. My stomach sank because the rosary was scheduled for 6:00, and it was 5:15, according to the clock on the wall. I was out of the apartment, flying. But the wind sent me into streets and alleys I didn't want to go down. I tightened my stomach and pushed with all my might. I got there "Chicano time," late.

The Everlasting Light Mortuary didn't appear to live up to its name. The corners of the building were hammered open in search of termites. *Dawg,* I thought, *I'm going to be buried in a coffin eaten by termites?* I hoped that my mom and dad had ordered a metal casket. But I had nothing to joke about when I walked through the termite-infested walls and saw my family and friends, a few lingering around the coffin where my body lay. Candles sputtered, incense hung in the air. Organ music droned out of a cracked speaker. The termites got to snack on the woofers, too.

The rosary, it appeared, was over, but not the grief. My mom was crying, and some aunts I hadn't seen in years were tossing tears freely. Uncle Richard was there, along with his girlfriend, who in her high heels was taller than him and just about every guy in the room. Then I spotted the four Js—Jamal had a middle finger in a splint, a basketball injury. Jason sported a bruise under his eye, also an injury. I felt good for them because their appearance suggested that we had won over Sanger. Coach wouldn't have put them in if the game had been close. After all, they were second stringers.

"Hey, guys," I greeted, but, of course, they couldn't hear or see me. Still, I thought I'd better greet them. They were huddled together, segregated from the adults because they were young. I was going to miss them, and I think they were going to miss me, too, at least until I became a photo in a yearbook, *nada más,* or in ten years' time a name mentioned at a high school reunion.

I remember when I was little I had ruined the classroom pencil sharpener when I stuck a crayon in and gave it a mighty crank. The teacher called Mom, and Mom called Dad, and Dad, home from work, called me from the backyard, where I was playing with Angel. My *nalga* whipping took me from the living room to the bedroom and back to the living room. I remembered crying in my bedroom, rain on the window, and thinking that if I died they would be really, really sorry. I was seven at the time, so full of self-pity that I pictured them at my funeral, all crying because they missed me. *See?* I sniveled back then.

You should have been nice to me. Given me more candy!
Taken me places! I didn't mean to break the sharpener!

It had come true. They were crying at my funeral and whether they were thinking they should have been nicer to me, *pues*, I wasn't able to tell for sure. But those were real tears. And the body in the coffin was real, too. I approached it slowly and almost buckled because I was full of self-pity.

"Oh, Chuy," I heard someone call. "Oh, Jesús!"

It was Aunt Sara from Modesto. With a raccoon look from the mascara on her face, she returned to view my body once again. She honked into a Kleenex and her husband ushered her away. When she was gone, I stepped forward. I swallowed my fear as I lowered my gaze to the body in the coffin. It was me, after all. I was dressed in a new black suit and a tie that was the colors of my school, black and red. My hands, laced together, rested on my stomach. I realized that I wasn't too *feo*-looking, even with my large nose. My hair was combed nice, but my cheeks had too much makeup! There was nothing I could do about that, though. I couldn't do anything about the little smirk on my face. I was smirking as if Angel was in the middle of a joke and I was lifting the corners of my mouth ready to laugh.

I did laugh. *Dawg!* I barked to myself. Me in my coffin with a grin on my face. I had to wonder whether it was going to relax or if I would have to wear it as I was lowered into the ground, where I would spin and spin with the daily rotation of the earth.

I turned and eyed my *primo* Eddie shoving something large and heavy into my mom's hands. My mom tried to give it back, but Eddie—bless him— wouldn't have it. It was back in my mom's care. The world was safer, quieter. I only prayed that someone would roll my coffin away before the termites got a chance to burrow into the polished wood of my snug little bed.

But I had had enough of these dark thoughts. I wanted more from life, even if I didn't have one. I wanted something to really remember.

CHAPTER
Nine

THE COLISEUM in Oakland was jammed with cars, trucks, campers, and Harley-Davidson motorcycles. Small barbecues were fired up, sending spirals of smoke into a sky lit by banks of lights. Ice chests brimmed with sodas and beers, and, at one site, champagne—someone with class and better breeding than most of the dudes at the game was ready to celebrate a victory. I watched a guy bringing a taco bloated as a water balloon to his face. Juice ran down an arm decorated with a bluish Raiders tattoo. He could have chosen the name of a girlfriend or wife who could disappear in a huff. But the Raiders? They were permanent.

On that Sunday night I asked myself what I would really like besides snuggling in the arms of Crystal. The answer was clear as the puddles I stepped over: to see a Raiders game live, not on TV. It was a simple gift to myself. Luck had it that the Raiders were playing on *Monday Night Football.*

That Sunday, as I drifted around Fresno, I found myself on Fausto's block. I thought maybe Robert Montgomery followed Yellow Shoes there. *Robert might want to go with me,* I thought. But Robert wasn't there, or Fausto, whose house was blown wide open. After I froze off the hinges of the front door, the *mocoso* kids in the neighborhood had sneaked in and taken off with the bikes. Even the ones with flats and no wheels.

"Incredible," I muttered.

Two kids were bike riding at the late hour of nine o'clock when they should have been bathed and buttoned up in bed. School was the next day. But they couldn't care less. The kids rode through rain puddles, their black, black hair parted by wind and drizzle. They were fearless.

After I had left the Everlasting Light Mortuary, I had walked in the rain and lamented my death. I was feeling sorry for myself and for Crystal, a girl I'd decided I truly loved. She was at home, perhaps watching her parents cry their hearts out until there were no tears left to race down their long, ashen faces. I had promised to return to her, and I was going to keep my word, which was the only thing I had left.

I ghosted around Fresno that Sunday night, and early the next morning, at a 7-Eleven, I slid into a van with three chubby guys—all *raza*—who were making plans to escape to Oakland. They worked for the city in sanitation, and decided to call in sick— let the garbage fester in the alleys. They wanted to see the Raiders play the Kansas City Chiefs, a rivalry that went back to the 1970s. Back then the Raiders had Stabler at the helm and Biletnikoff running a slow but effective pattern.

We departed Fresno a little after two o'clock in the afternoon. I rode with these guys, and for three hours straight they talked about what they were escaping: work. They talked about the good stuff people tossed in the garbage.

"The garbage I handle is first-rate," a guy named Hector bragged. He worked a route in the best part of Fresno and had taken away, cleaned up and repaired, and sold on his front lawn in a yard sale enough goods to put his son through the first year of college. City College, but still . . .

One guy named Manuel was bummed out. His route was in the poorer parts of Fresno, and he never got anything worth salvaging. Even the pork chops were gnawed to the bone, so his dog never feasted on other people's scraps. The cereal boxes were cleaned out, the egg and milk cartons, the soup cans, *todo*!

There was no waste in the area he worked. Times were hard, and getting harder. Even the flies were disappointed.

They took an inventory of things they had gaffled, and the people who lived on their routes. Hector bragged that there was a woman who liked him, and the others taunted, "Is she blind?" Their laughter rattled the bag of barbecue pork rinds in their laps.

Near Livermore my name came up—or, to be truthful, my murder.

"You hear about that *chavalo* who got stabbed?" Manuel asked. His forehead became pinched with hurt.

"Yeah," Hector muttered. "I'd kill the dude that killed my son." He was looking out the window at a subdivision of new homes that were going up, their frames like gallows, the tiled roofs the color of dried blood. "Kids got it harder now than when we were running the streets."

"You got that right," agreed Manuel.

The three drove in silence the rest of the way. But as the bright lights of the Oakland Coliseum appeared against the gray sky, the gang of three— even the one at the wheel—started to slip into their Raiders gear—hats, jerseys, black under their eyes as if they were players. They didn't moan when parking cost fifteen dollars and scalped tickets set them back eighty each. They were there to party.

My friends went one way, and I went another, hugging the ground because I was almost being blown away by the wind off the bay. I took in the sights of a pre-game party in the huge parking lot that surrounded the stadium. I had no hunger but appreciated others who stomped their shoes and boots when they dipped a tortilla chip in salsa and couldn't handle the fiery taste. I couldn't catch the footballs that were tossed around the parking lot, and the dudes playing catch couldn't catch them, either. The dogs that ran barking had more natural gifts for catching Frisbees than the middle-aged jocks with sausages for fingers.

The wind slashed through the parking lot. I decided to float over the fans entering the gates of the Coliseum. I was tripped out by the size of the place, and by the fans wigged out in Raiders gear—one guy had a skull on each bulky shoulder. The skulls were more handsome than he was, I swear. He had no front teeth, and his eyes were sunk deep into his flesh. His nostrils were large as nickels.

It was six days before Halloween, but every Sunday—Monday in this case—was Halloween for the Raiders Nation. Everyone wore black, and almost everyone made a fashion statement with masks, skulls, chains, shields, tiny spears, body plates of rippled muscle, flags, the whole nine yards, as my dad would say. If you came dressed in a simple sweater, you were out of place. If you had manners, you may as well go home.

I found myself a front-row seat. The Raiderettes were doing a routine to a song I couldn't place. I thought of Crystal, a former cheerleader. If she had been at my side, she would snarl at the Raiderettes and maybe jealously call them a name or two. I would call them "sweet" or "hot," the vocabulary of a seventeen-year-old boy. How else was I supposed to respond?

"This is sweet," I said to myself when the Raiders won the toss and chose to receive the kick-off. The Chiefs lined up, kicked off, and the game began with a fumble. The fans moaned but none booed. Only sixteen seconds had been chewed off the clock. *What was the big deal?* the fans thought. But the Chiefs, three plays later, scored on a quarterback keeper.

A guy, chest bare and face painted black-and-white, raced down the aisle and roared next to me, "That call suuuuuuucks!" He was practicing for the bad calls the refs would make. He bared his feelings again when security escorted him away.

I realized that because I was invisible, I could move down to the bench where players were gargling on Gatorade and being taped up by assistants.

"Tonto!" I scolded myself. "Get down there on the field."

I dived from the stands and was picked up by the wind that swirled burger wrappers. I sailed and hung over the fans in primo seats, the ones close to the field that cost a fortune, before landing a few feet from the Raiders head coach, who was rolling a Life Saver in his mouth. He was taller than I imagined, and suddenly angry as he slapped his clipboard on his thigh. He crunched the Life Saver into a sweet dust. His brow furrowed as the offensive coordinator up in the booth called a play. However, the head coach vetoed that play and called his own, his hand in front of his face. But I picked up his body language. It was a running play because his right arm went to his chest as if he were huddling the rock.

I was right. The running back gained six yards on a straight-ahead play that was all power and grit. The running back jumped up and ran off the field because his shoe had kicked off. Right then I looked down at where my feet should have been. They were long gone, as were my legs. My arms had vanished, too. My favorite part of my body—my abs— was going fuzzy. I tried to wipe out this sour image of myself. I was there to see the Raiders win!

"Come on, guys!" I crowed.

They adjusted their jocks and helmets, and stuck

their mouthpieces back into their chops. They held hands in the huddle, and there was nothing girlie about that. Even from the sidelines I could see that they were huge and would have had trouble getting into Uncle Richard's Honda.

I gazed up at one of the booths, where the offensive coordinator was making the calls. *What a job!* I thought. I sized up the cheerleaders, pom-poms flailing, who were dancing to the Stones' "Start Me Up." I even liked the goofy guy in the stands shouting "Popcorn!" I would have loved that job, or even the job sweeping up the popcorn that didn't make it to the fans' mouths. No telling what I would have found as I swept up after one long, drunken party.

I drifted out onto the field. Who was there to stop me? After a field goal—the Raiders were stopped on the seventeen-yard line—I sailed out to the center of the fifty-yard line, which was already torn up by spiked shoes. I hovered near the kicker as he squeezed the football and placed it on the upright. I turned and scanned the sidelines, where the players, exhausted from the last play, were bent over and breathing, their white breath hanging in the autumn sky. And it was a lovely sight seeing a player throw up. Where else could I witness a player playing his guts out?

I turned back as the kicker sent the ball; it sailed

into the lights and seemed to hang on the roar of the crowd. Then it tumbled end over end, and the defensive team, helmets lowered, started a fearless charge up the field. I flew with them, eyes wide-open for at least ten yards. I blinked, however, when a Chief with bloodshot eyes and hot snot blowing from his nostrils ran right through me. If I had been flesh and bone, I would have been out for a long time. These guys could hurt. Even their looks stung, and especially the slashing fury in their eyes.

A ref whistled, threw a yellow flag into the air, and called a foul by the Raiders. The fifteen-yard penalty had the culprit, hands on hips, wagging his head at the injustice of being picked on. But I saw him smiling in his helmet that barely fit his large head. He fit his mouthpiece back in and was ready for more of the same.

I huddled with the Raiders. Some numbers were called, and I didn't understand what was what. The Chiefs ran a run to the left and got nowhere. With the next play, the tight end of the Chiefs fumbled the rock and the Raiders smothered it.

A roar burst forth from the soul of every man and woman who wanted to go home winners. They wanted a good memory of the evening, something to say tomorrow at work, "Yeah, I was there last night. Stacked up the Chiefs good." That roar had a powerful spirit to it, and it sent me sailing from the Coliseum. I rose laughing, rose tumbling like a poorly thrown football, rose and slowly descended into the parking lot. I had seen enough.

I FELT HAPPY and had no regrets about missing the second half of the game. The wind hoisted me away from the Coliseum. I flew toward Fresno, feeling giddy. Over the Altamont Ridge two geese appeared out of nowhere and were winging at my side. We flew in formation, with me in the lead by a couple of feet.

"You're cool birds," I praised, and they honked at me. The geese were slick, long-necked, and beautiful to watch because at times they would dip into the darkness of night only to reappear when we passed over the lights of the many farms we passed. How they could find me, a ghost, was a mystery. But they flew at my side, guiding me home.

Fresno was a hundred miles away, too long for me to fly, and I got as far as Los Baños before I tired and said good-bye to the geese, who continued their flight south. There, at ten at night, I hooked a ride with a gray-haired husband and wife and listened to religious music all the way to Belmont Avenue. I lolled in the backseat of their car, which not only obeyed the speed limit, but crawled to Fresno, they were so slow. The wife, Dolores, opened a Thermos and poured hot coffee into its red plastic lid. The husband thanked her with a smile, and I had to smile. Here was a perfect marriage, and here was a music that blessed our journey, for it seemed every other word sung was *Jesus*.

CHAPTER
Ten

Tuesday morning. The sky was gray as eraser markings on paper. I loitered in front of Saint John's Cathedral. The pigeons were warbling in the eaves, and a priest was tiptoeing out of the parish house and down the cold and damp steps. He was retrieving the *Fresno Bee*. *He might be saying my mass,* I thought. It would not be an easy day for him.

I went inside the church and made my way to the altar, where I said a made-up prayer for Crystal, whom I loved more than ever. I have to admit that I prayed for the Raiders. They had lost after all, and their fans were now waking up with dark bags under their eyes. The poor sanitation crew was at work already, their hands gloved and rolling cans to the hungry mouth of the garbage truck idling in an alley.

"Jesus," I asked. "Jesus, do we come back?" I shivered and let out a tearless cry that jerked my shoulders. I told Him that I loved my family and Angel, Eddie my cousin, Uncle Richard, my friends at school, and those people I never met because I had died young. What would I miss? What wars, conflicts, or miracle drugs that might bring back a teenage boy dying from knife wounds? "Please, God," I begged, "take care of my parents." I was an only son, and would miss the passing of my parents. Perhaps I would see them in the afterlife. *God, make it so,* I prayed in front of an altar that was lit by a single sputtering candle.

I closed my eyes and imagined the paintings of the saints on the fifty-foot ceiling, which was cracked and rain-stained in places. When I was in elementary school, Mom took me to mass every Sunday, and every Sunday I yawned until the mist of boredom pressed against my eyes. What intrigued me was how the artist got up to the tall, tall ceiling to do his thing. How did he climb up there? Or did someone tie a rope around his waist and haul him there, swinging side to side like a pendulum? Did they have a ladder so tall that it entered the *Guinness Book of Records*? Or scaffolds put together like Legos? The artist could have crawled through the roof and poked his head here and there to paint those saintly drawings. That's how I spent my time in church, in wonderment.

I got up, turned, and discovered Yellow Shoes, head down and in prayer at the back of the church. Candles flickered behind him, and I thought of those candles as pilot lights for the flames he would have to dance around for eternity. In hell an angry God would turn up the flames and roast this gang banger forever and ever.

"*Cabrón,*" I muttered, and immediately felt guilty for cussing in church. I told God that I was sorry as I bowed my head and whispered, "Forgive me, *Señor.*" I approached Yellow Shoes, who looked up with a smile that was crooked on his face, like he wasn't used to smiling and was first learning how to be happy. I thought for a moment that he could see me, that he was mocking me.

"What are you laughing at, *pendejo?*" I yelled.

Yellow Shoes rose to his feet and greeted me in a brotherly voice, "How are you?" He should have known the answer to that. He extended his hand as a sign of peace.

Spooked, I flowed backward and hung momentarily in the air. Out of the corner of my eye, I saw one of the saints staring at me, judging my reaction. I didn't understand Yellow Shoes's sudden kindness in the shape of the hand beckoning for friendship.

"Chihuahua!" I yelled.

A ghostly face started to rise from Yellow Shoes's shoulder, then the neck, torso, and rest of the body. It was Robert Montgomery. Had he been inside Yellow Shoes since I last saw him on the bus?

"Chuy," Robert greeted. He pretended not to be disturbed that most of my body had vanished and all that remained was my upper torso and head. But I could read the sadness in his eyes. He was feeling for me.

"You scared me!"

Robert laughed. He laughed harder as Yellow Shoes looked around the church, confused at why he was there with his hand extended. "Jesus," he called, but I didn't believe that God was going to answer him. He quickly rose, closed his hands into fists, and ran out of the church, with his *huango* pants and his *chones* showing. He was running, and from what I knew of him, he would be running all his life, a coward with blood on his hands.

"I was trying to steer this guy right," he said, pointing with his stumps. His hands had already disappeared. He didn't seem scared. "You know, I thought that if I was inside him I could work his movements a little. Get him to behave and not be such a punk." He shook his head. "I guess I was wrong."

148

"How did you know that I was going to be here?" I asked.

Sorrow shone in his eyes. "I just knew," he answered, and staring at the font of holy water confessed, "I know your funeral is going to be here." He buried his face in his stumps and his shoulders shook. He was crying for me. He sat down in the pew, then kneeled.

I lifted my gaze toward the ceiling. How did the painter paint up there?

"I used to go to church here," I told Robert.

"Yeah, me, too."

"Really?"

He rubbed his face with his right stump, a sign that he was going to tell me something funny. "Actually, I used to sleep here. But it got spooky looking up at the ceiling and seeing all those saints watching me."

We admired those paintings that hung high up in the cold shadows.

"Man, I don't know how someone could paint way up," Robert said after a moment.

My face brightened. Others, it seemed, had the same question.

"I used to work as a painter," Robert told me. "Painted houses throughout all of Fresno." He giggled. "I dated a gal who asked me to paint her garage. I painted the house, and she gave me the boot before the house could dry."

"That's sorry," I lamented. But I had to admit that it was funny.

His smile evaporated. Robert stepped toward me, gave me a hug and foretold the future. "I'll see you again." His face was lined with grief. "Thanks for saving my life. I should have done better. A lot better, even if I was a terrible housepainter." He turned away and headed toward the altar. He had to speak to God on his own.

Should have done better, I mused as I approached the heavy oak doors of the church and floated through with ease. I think I understood.

Outside, with the wind blowing, I had a hard time keeping myself on the ground. I was like a balloon in the wind. I sailed and descended, and bounced one way and another. Once I righted myself, I grew scared.

A man in a khaki gardening outfit was setting an iron sign in the gutter in front of the church. The sign read: FUNERAL.

I HEARD MY middle-grade English teacher use the word *afterlife* when she told us about this poet named Dante and the rings of hell he had to go down. I didn't think anything of its meaning and how after we die there is a chance that we might enjoy yet another life. *Who cares?* I argued to myself, as I used a dried-up Bic pen to scratch my name on the top of my desk. I wanted to make sure that I left behind my *placa,* my name, so that others would understand that I ruled that desk for a year. So what if I got a C in English that semester? What a *mocoso* I was in seventh grade!

And it didn't make sense for Peter, a friend from fifth grade, to confess to me that the day after his father died—a tractor rolled over him as he was plowing rows to plant cotton—he'd heard his dad's footsteps on the gravel in his front yard. We were in a tree, and it was autumn, like now, close to Halloween because I remember that we were eating pumpkin seeds that his mother had roasted in the oven. We were in the tree only because it was something to do. Dawg, we were dumb. We were excited to chirp stupidly, like birds in a tree that had been stripped of most of its leaves, though two bird nests, cold and abandoned, remained lodged in the crotch of limbs. We had climbed the tree to size up our neighborhood, eat our pumpkin seeds, and, I guess, after pretending to be chirping birds, allow Peter to talk about his dad, who was from Mexico, a hard worker with hands like roots pulled from the earth.

That was ten years ago. We straddled the limbs of that ancient sycamore, talked, and watched the sun dip bloodred behind a feathery cloud. I thought of Peter as I left Saint John's and about the word *afterlife*. I was almost gone. I had died when I was seventeen, and what had I done with my life? Saved a man named Robert Montgomery, who in the end died anyhow. But that was something, no? I had also gone door-to-door collecting money for research to cure cerebral palsy, seven years straight. That, too, was something.

At home, I didn't give my parents much grief. I had been a good kid, though Dad had to chase me with his belt a couple of times. Even my mom got into the action when I did something wrong and she couldn't wait for Dad to come home. With the flat of her hand poised to strike, she chased me around the kitchen table.

A block away from Saint John's Cathedral, I heard a garbage truck braking and then the roar of the driver yelling "Stop!"—he was one of the guys who had unwittingly given me a ride to Oakland to see the game. His name was Manuel, I remembered. He was happily whistling, though there were bags under his eyes. His face was recklessly shaven and crusted with blood where he had nicked himself, perhaps out of punishment for taking a day off to see the Raiders lose. He stopped momentarily when he came across the sign that read FUNERAL. I could see him think about that sign. His whistling stopped and his face became seamed with dark lines. He considered the sign and then continued down the walkway between the parish house and the cathedral. There was garbage to pick up.

I flew from there on a wind that was as sharp as a knife, and cold. I headed south toward Selma to hook up with Crystal. A romantic, I was loving her in my heart more and more. *We'll be together in the afterlife,* I thought, and as I was carried along by the wind that seemed to be spanking me, I admonished myself for not listening to my English teacher talk about that guy Dante. *Tonto,* I scolded myself.

I passed Jensen Avenue, with its lots full of lines and lines of diesel trucks and farm equipment for sale, and glided up Highway 99, lined with oleanders whipped by the traffic's wind. Tumbleweeds were caught in the barbed wire fences, and strips of blown truck tires littered the shoulders of the highway. A treasure of broken bottles and crushed soda cans gleamed in the weeds. There were flattened suitcases, Styrofoam ice chests, folding chairs, lamps, and broken-apart sofas—stuff that fell off the backs of pickups. I came across an occasional dead dog and poor, homeless dudes who looked like dead dogs. At the entrances to the highway, they were holding up hitchhiking signs that would take them south to Los Angeles. Fresno was too hard on the homeless.

I cut west from the freeway and, suddenly, I was flying over vineyards and pastures where cows looked dully at the ground, drool like clear string hanging from their fly-flecked mouths. I passed sheep, too, and chicken coops. I took a quick break when I spotted a llama farm.

Dawg, I thought as I approached that exotic animal. I had seen llamas in books, but never one close up. Their mouths chewed, but they weren't eating anything. They just chewed and chewed, and scratched the hard ground with their hooves. Then one of them spit an orange gob in my direction. If I had had feet, they would have gotten wet. Then, as if to make a further comment about me, the llama lifted its tail and dropped four marble-sized turds that steamed in the morning light.

"You furry little *cochino!*" I scolded, then laughed.

I leaped and the wind carried me southward toward Selma and over vineyards and ranch homes. I flew across the bullet-riddled sign that announced Selma, Raisin Capital of the World, and spotted Crystal's house. I slowed my flight because I could make out Crystal's father on their front porch. His head was down and at first I believed he was crying because his shoulders were jerking. As I got closer I saw that I was wrong. He was pulling up a rusty nail with fingers as thick and callused as my dad's. His daughter was dead and, I guess, he was keeping busy. In his mind, the rusty nail had to go.

Three cars were in the driveway, and I suspected one was an unmarked police cruiser. It just had that look. But I was wrong there, too, because soon the front door opened and a man in a black suit came out, briefcase in hand. The briefcase seemed to weigh a lot, because the man's shoulder was slumped from carrying it. I realized immediately who he was. He was the man from a funeral home, and he had just conducted business with Crystal's dad and mom. Maybe he brought out brochures about caskets and headstones. I feared the discussion.

Full of sorrow, I swung my attention away and stared absently at the vineyards, where a blackbird on a wire was wiping its beak under a wing. "Crystal," I moaned. The blackbird, done with its primping, leveled its wings and jumped, the wire like a guitar string producing a metallic twang.

"Chuy," I heard.

I turned. It was Crystal, coming out of the vineyard, and she did not seem in the least shocked that my body was nearly gone. But I was troubled that her legs—how beautiful they were—were gone, as were most of her arms. Her long, brownish hair flowed, and the corners of her mouth were dented with the start of a smile.

Crystal approached me with the stumps of her arms out. What a rare gift for an average-looking dude like me! To be the object of desire! Crystal leaned her face to mine and gave me a light kiss, then one that was heavier, for her tongue touched mine in greeting. We clunked our heads together, bashful as ponies.

"Crystal," I whispered, my face in her neck.

"Chuy," she said back in a sweet whisper.

We kissed again and touched nose to nose. Was a ghost ever so happy?

We laughed and then became quiet when the funeral man's car pulled away, raising a long cloud of farm dust. We watched the car stop at the end of the drive, its brake lights deep red against the grayish morning.

We looked toward the house when the front door closed with a click. Crystal's father was gone, and the blackbird that I had seen earlier settled on the rail. The bird cleaned itself again, but beat its wings and lifted skyward when the door opened. Crystal's mother, shrugging into a coat, came out. She shaded her eyes, as if she was looking for her daughter, and, not finding her, began to tend to a potted plant's dead petals. I let Crystal pull in all the images of her mother that she could. I watched her take in, as if for the last time, her mother's dark hair, her face, her hands methodically pinching at dead flowers. Her mother then shaded her eyes and stared far away.

"Oh, Mother," Crystal moaned.

I lowered my head. Two ants were carrying a feathery seed that was three times bigger than them. The little guys had courage and purpose.

I waited a patient five minutes before saying, "Let's go."

We turned, flowed a few inches from the ground, and found ourselves at the side of her house. Once more, I inspected the faucet where I had washed my face after the wasp stings. I gazed up at the barn, where the abandoned honeycomb nests mostly remained.

"Chuy," Crystal volunteered. "I missed you."

I swallowed that tender declaration.

"I missed you, too," I said. "God, I wish I knew—"

She cut me off, as if she could read my mind, and said, "But you know me now."

Our deaths would be remembered by family and a few friends who might think of us as they drove through the streets of Fresno and Selma. Let them remember us as okay kids—both of us long-distance runners who didn't get very far.

We leaped into the air and the wind took us.

"Where are we going?" Crystal asked. Her hair swirled in front of her face, which was pink from the cold wind.

I smiled at her. "Let's check it out," I answered without fear as we sailed over her farm and over a farm that was like hers, full of grapevines.

They say autumn is the color of death, and, for Crystal and me, it was true. We were like the tint of fallen leaves, grass burnt by the first frost, and the ashen-colored fog that sometimes rises from the valley floor and smothers our dreams. My dream had been to grow up, work a regular job, nothing special, hang out with friends, and be with someone special like Crystal. I received a portion of that dream and felt grateful for it. I loved her like no other. She flew at my side, southward toward what, I now knew, is called the afterlife.

Selected Spanish Words and Phrases

ay, dios	oh, God
borrachos	drunkards
cabrón	bastard
los campos	the countryside
cara	face
carnal	blood brother
chale	no way
chavalo	child
chicas	girls
chicharrones	pork rinds
chismosos/as	gossipers
cholo	gangster
chones	underpants
la chota	the police
churros	doughnut-like pastry
"Cielito Lindo"	a song

cochino	pig
comadre	extremely close woman friend
cruda	hangover
entiendes	understand
feo	ugly
feria	cash
hijole	wow
huango	loose, misshapen
mala	bad
menudo	a soup
mi'jo	my son
mi abuela	my grandmother
mi novia	my sweetheart
mi papi	my daddy
mocosos	snot-nosed kids
mota	marijuana
nada más	no more
nalgas	buttocks
novio	boyfriend
paleta	Popsicle
panadería	bakery
pan dulce	sweet bread
pendejo	stupid person
placa	signature graffiti
primo	cousin
pues	well
puta	whore

qué asco	how disgusting
qué gacho	what a mess/what a bad thing
quien sabe	who knows
rancheras	old-fashioned songs
raza	Latino race
sapo	toad
sin vergüenza	shameless
suave	cool
telenovela	soap opera
tonto	stupid
tripas	intestines
vato	cool guy
viejo	old man